THE

#1

RULE

FOR

GIRLS

Also by Rachel McIntyre
Me & Mr J

RACHEL McINTYRE

THE #1 RULE FOR GIRLS

First published in Great Britain in 2016
by Electric Monkey, an imprint of Egmont UK Limited
The Yellow Building, 1 Nicholas Road, London W11 4AN

Text copyright © 2016 Rachel McIntyre
The moral rights of the author have been asserted

ISBN 978 1 4052 7345 9

58096/1

www.egmont.co.uk

A CIP catalogue record for this title is available from the British Library

Typeset by Avon DataSet Ltd, Bidford on Avon, Warwickshire
Printed and bound in Great Britain by CPI Group

For Christina Kiley

CHAPTER 1

I was ripping the firelighters open when Ayesha arrived.

'What the . . .?' She peered down at the barbecue. 'Oh, Daisy, please tell me that's not your school uniform.'

'I'm making a Symbolic Gesture,' I said, placing my tie on top of the pile.

She tutted as she picked up my blazer. 'Man-made fabrics don't burn, they *melt*. And what about the buttons and zips? Why couldn't you take it to a charity shop, like a normal person?'

'Because I need to rise from the ashes of these polyester school chains,' I said as I picked up the matches. 'To be reborn to a new life at sixth-form college. A phoenix —'

But she'd already gone to the back door to ask my mum for a plastic bag.

Now *Beth* would've been up for my sacrificial inferno; crazy, impulsive yin to Ayesha's sensible yang that she was. But according to Facebook she was out somewhere 'feeling excited' with her new boyfriend.

Fast-forward half an hour and we were sitting on a bus heaving with Saturday shoppers. As we pulled into the station, Ayesha looked up and down the street.

'Aha,' she said, flapping her hand at a green shopfront. 'How about that one?'

The idea of going back to St Mary's had been depressing me for weeks. Since the day Matt dumped me in fact. So donating my school uniform to the Samaritans . . .?

'Perfect,' I said, stepping on to the pavement, the bag containing my old life clutched tightly in my hand.

'Are you absolutely certain this is what you want?' Ayesha asked as we crossed the road. 'You're sure you don't want to stay on at school with me and Beth?'

'No chance,' I said, symbolically dumping my blazer, tie, skirt, scarf – the whole hideous shebang – in the shop doorway. 'I've made up my mind. I am never going back.'

Later that evening, I had just endured one of Mum's experimental dinners (like gravel fried in sweat) when

Beth rang me in a full on 'my parents hate my boyfriend' meltdown.

I SWEAR I didn't set out to be unsympathetic. I mean, I was no stranger to the agony of man trouble myself. But honestly I'd heard these dating stories so many times before they were practically, you know, *biblical*.

And on the first day Beth meeteth a crap man,

And this man was a total wasteth of time,

And Beth cryeth. A lot.

And the more she ranted the more I found myself almost siding with her mum and dad.

Actually, make that *totally* siding.

OK, so I hadn't met her new boyfriend yet. But no matter how much I got to know him I'd never be able to unknow these two disturbing facts:

1. How they met. (She walked past him in her school uniform and *he followed her home*.)
2. His mates called her 'jailbait'.

According to Ayesha, he was a bouncer. With a tattoo on his neck. Which was spelled wrong.

Not exactly *Romeo and Juliet* then. And Beth's dad

(aka High Priest of the Victorian Dads' Club) couldn't know these creepy finer details either or she'd have been gagged, bound and shackled, never mind merely grounded.

So less than a minute into Beth's rantathon and I was already in a mental tug of war. Should I make the supportive 'poor you' noises she'd be expecting or say what I really thought?

'Dad can't see past Shaney's job,' Beth was saying now. 'I told him it's standing on the door of The Rat and Drainpipe, not dealing drugs to toddlers. And anyway it's only while he figures out what he really wants to do.'

This definitely called for diplomacy.

'Well, I suppose it must be difficult to find jobs with his, er, literacy issues,' I said.

'What "literacy issues"?'

'Ayesha mentioned the tattoo,' I said.

Beth tutted. Loudly. 'GOD, how many times! There's nothing wrong with Shaney's spelling, it was the tattooist's fault.'

Oops, I'd obviously touched a nerve there. 'Sorry. Didn't realise.'

There was a moment's silent huff before she hit back. 'So, have you spoken to Matt yet?'

My heart thudded, like it always did when someone said his name.

'No. He dumped me and moved to Spain. Remember?'

'Don't be so touchy, I was only asking,' she said. 'It's so ridiculous you two aren't talking. You need to ring him and sort it out.'

Relationship advice from Queen of the Waster Chasers? *As if*.

I said a very frosty 'gotta go' and lay back on my bed. I just didn't understand: if my friends and family really wanted to help me get over Matt, why did they keep talking about him? No one seemed to get it: even if his mum's bar failed and he crawled home from Magaluf on bleeding knees wearing nothing but horsehair underpants and a hat made of brambles . . . I'd still say bollocks to him.

Swipe left school. Swipe left Matt. It was time to move on.

Because as Shaney's tattoo said: *You only live wonce*.

CHAPTER 2

'I am *soooo* jealous,' Ayesha said as she peered in my wardrobe.

'Jealous clothes or jealous there's no uniform at college?' I asked, adding yet another cardigan to the pile on my bed.

'Both.' She sighed.

As some ancient Greek guy probably never said, no one gets a second chance to make a first impression and so choosing the perfect outfit for my induction at college required careful consideration and help in the form of Ayesha the Wise.

She was assessing the skirts now, taking each one out of the wardrobe and holding it up. 'You've got so many lovely things, Daze. You're so lucky.'

Yep, I totally got the clothes envy. My mum was a

professional seamstress. Ayesha's mum was a chiropodist. My house: piles of to-die-for clothes. Ayesha's house: piles of manky foot bits.

'Beth rang me in tears about whatshisname, Tattoo Tosser,' I said, rattling coat hangers down the rail. 'You know her dad's locked her in the coal shed? Mouldy crusts for dinner, hourly spankings with the family Bible.'

'It's not funny,' said Ayesha. 'She's been really upset all day.'

'So what's Shaney like then?' I said. 'Apart from dyslexic.'

'Into leather.'

'Kinky?'

She shook her head. 'Motorbikes.'

'No wonder Beth's dad's gone mental,' I said.

'I know. And we thought she'd scraped the barrel when she met Stinky Pete.'

I nodded slowly. Ah yes, Stinky Pete. Beth's beardy, battle-re-enacting ex-boyf who dressed like a Viking at the weekends . . . and washed like a Viking at all other times. She finally hung up her horns after an unexpectedly warm spell in March, telling him he needed to spend less time in costume and more time with Mr Soap.

She was pulling dresses out of the wardrobe now and

arranging them on top of my bed.

'So what's the deal?' I asked.

'Well, he does weightlifting so he's got these massive muscles. She says he makes her feel girly.'

Girly. I flashed on a vision of Beth pinked up, giggly and fluffified. Scattering IQ points like confetti every time Shaney flexed a bicep because she'd fallen for the myth that fit guys never fancy clever girls.

'Sounds like she scraped through the bottom of the barrel this time,' I said.

'Er, what happened to Rule number 2?' said Ayesha. 'You know — *Always support your friends.*'

Ah, yes. The Rules were how me, Beth and Ayesha first got to know each other. It was during one of those get-to-know-the-group things at the start of Year 7: come up with a list of rules of acceptable behaviour. I couldn't remember anything else we did in English that year, but the Rules stuck.

They were our Ten Commandments; the girl code our friendship was founded on. Except there were only nine of them. And they weren't so much carved in stone as totally rewritten in Year 9 when rules concerning boys became necessary. Still, the principle had stayed the same and, whenever I didn't know what to do, the

Rules could usually point me in the right direction.

It was actively depressing. Beth had the brains of a Nobel Prizewinner-in-waiting, but when it came to potential partners her man-nav was permanently set to 'unworthy'. And when the latest Mr OK turned out to be just another Mr No Way, me and Ayesha were left mopping up the tears and chanting Rule #3: *Never change to please someone else.*

'These?' Ayesha the fashion fairy held out a grey-and-fuchsia tea dress in one hand, a purple patterned blazer dangling from the other.

'Not too OTT?'

'No,' she said. 'You told me the best thing about college is that you can wear what you want . . . so, Rule number 6: *Dress to make yourself happy.*'

True. I had been poised to set fire to the Polyester Chains of Conformity the other day. Hardly a grand gesture then if I rose like a phoenix wearing tatty tracky bums and a band tee.

'You are so right, Mistress of the Wardrobe,' I said, getting out my nail polish collection. Hmmmm. Which to choose . . . *Dirty Liar* or *Shattered Soul*?

'Mock away.' She hung the dress on the door. 'But you are going to rock that college. Are you still dead excited?'

9

'I. Cannot. Wait.' I flicked through the Castlefields Sixth Form prospectus, stopping at a page stuffed with eye-wateringly pretty boys and girls. 'Look at that lot. Fresh out of teen heaven, not like the geeks at St Mary's. No offence.'

She squinted at the pictures. 'You do realise they're models?'

I waved the two nail-polish bottles at her. 'Which one?'

'The pink, to match your boots.' She gestured with the brochure then stuck it right under my nose. 'They've got to be models. Real people don't have teeth that glow in the dark.' She sighed. 'You could've stayed on at school, even if Matt has moved to Spain. You'd still have me and Beth.'

'I know,' I said. 'But I really need a fresh start.'

'I'm just worried you're rushing into it because you're cut up over Matt.'

I shook the bottle of *Dirty Liar* till it rattled. 'I'm completely over him, I promise. You could still come with me, you know. Listen.' I gazed down at the open brochure and read out loud. '*Make exciting new friends in an environment where individuality is celebrated and students are treated as adults.*'

'Yeah, it sounds great, but what can I say?' She

shrugged. 'I'm a St Mary's geek. I love it there. And you going to college won't change us being mates, will it? We'll still see each other at footie training and go out at the weekends and stuff.'

'That won't ever change,' I said passionately. 'The mess I was in this summer after Matt dumped me . . . well, you kept me from total meltdown. I literally wouldn't have coped without you.'

'He didn't dump you,' she said gently. 'You dumped him.'

'Yeah, but it was his decision to go, so technically he did the breaking up,' I reminded her. 'I just put it into words: me or Spain. And it's true, you mean the world to me.' There was a catch in my voice as I continued. 'If I thought it meant we wouldn't see each other, there's no way I'd have enrolled at Castlefields.'

'Oh, Daisy,' she said, putting her arms round me. 'It doesn't matter if we're not at the same school, you're not dumping me. I do understand why you want to start over, you know. And thick and thin, richer and poorer, and all that, I will always be there for you. I'm never going anywh—' She lifted my wrist to check my watch. 'Oh my God, look at the time! Sorry, Mum's got a fungal nail infection coming round and she needs me to swab.'

And off she went, pulling her coat on as I followed her downstairs.

I shut the door then wandered to the kitchen where I was subjected to a hideous experience, courtesy of my beloved parents.

I'd have poured bleach down my ears if I'd thought it would work, but *what's heard cannot be unheard* in the words of Lady Macbeth (possibly). It was only seven o'clock and Mum and Dad were already halfway through a bottle of *El Vino Blabbio*. Luckily my little brother, River, was safely tucked up in bed and thus spared the sight of his parents treading the merry path to total pixilation.

And their flimsy excuse?

Dad: 'Cheers! (*chinking glass with Mum's*) I can't believe our baby girl's all grown up and starting college. Seems like two minutes since she was — (*gestures matchbox-sized infant*).

Mum: (*soppy smile at Dad*) 'We did a good job, didn't we?'

Dad: (*soppy smile; grabs Mum's hand*) 'We certainly did, Susie. We proved them all wrong.'

Mum: 'Your nana's face when we told her we were expecting you, Daisy. I thought she was going to explode.'

Dad: 'Everyone said we'd never make a go of it, but here we are.'

Mum: 'And I wouldn't change a single second.' (*They look at each other and the room melts away.*)

Aww. Mum and Dad were the real love deal: school sweethearts to lifelong soulmates. Just like me and Matt in fact. (Minus the breaking up. And the moving to another country. And the never speaking to each other again.)

Dad: (*sigh*) 'Just kids ourselves, when you came along, love.'

Yes, the same age as me now and with the life of a miniature human being in their hands. Even though I was the happy result, the idea freaked me out. A baby at sixteen? I couldn't be trusted with a pot plant.

Mum: (*with a tipsy giggle*) 'Up to all sorts of hanky-panky, weren't we, Nick? Oooh, Daze, you wouldn't *believe* —'

Avoid! I put my fingers in my ears and started belting out *Singalonga Frozen* to deflect the way-too-much information coming at me. But even so, odd phrases filtered through the noise. Such as 'Harvey's birthday party', 'on that pile of coats', 'nine months to the day'.

Practically hyperventilating with embarrassment, I fled back up to my room.

Let it gooooo.

Knowing my parents were the definition of true love was wonderful. Picturing them engaged in 'hanky-panky'? *Ugh.*

My headphones helped to drown out the tipsy giggling floating up through the floorboards, but they couldn't stop my brain flashing up very unwelcome images. Oh God, I was NEVER letting them within sniffing distance of a cork again.

<u>(The very, very end of) Daisy Green's To-do List</u>
- Item 2,301: Lick inside of wheelie bin.
- Item 2,302: Nail foot to bedroom floor.
- Item 2,303: Visualise circumstances of own conception.

How come when I needed to remember important stuff (such as maths), my mind went blank. But when I was desperate to *forget* something (parental confessions; Matt breaking up with me), I had the memory of an elephant with a PhD in Photographic Recall.

Like now. Lying in bed with that awful moment playing like a Vine.

I'm sorry, Daisy, but I'm going to Spain. Loop. *I'm sorry,*

Daisy, but I'm going to Spain. Loop. *I'm sorry, Daisy, but I'm going to Spain.* Loop.

That six-second conversation had been a constant background hum since the day we broke up. Every now and then, something would happen to turn the volume up. Maybe a song; or a whiff of aftershave; or a YouTube clip he'd almost wet his pants over; or River asking for the bazillionth time when Matt was coming home. And that's when it hit me like the first time. My legs always shook, throat burned, stomach went all peculiar and I couldn't quite trust my ears. You're *leaving* me? You're going to live in *Spain*? To help your mum and stepdad open a *bar*?

I'd have to sit down, take a few deep breaths. Maybe cry, maybe not, depending who was around. Wait until it faded into the background again. *I'm sorry, Daisy, but I'm going to Spain* endlessly looping.

OK. College had to be the answer. A new start. I could get up and put my happy mask on. Try to act as if my heart didn't dissolve out of my tear ducts every night.

Queen of Pretend. Fake as a reality TV star. Tomorrow my post-Matt reboot would begin, my big chance to move on.

Rule #8: *Think positive.* I'd never needed it more.

CHAPTER 3

Okaaaay. So I'd been there, done that, and by 4 o'clock I just needed the *Hang on, this isn't what the brochure promised* T-shirt to make the college induction day complete.

Where were the many 'exciting new friends' I was supposed to be making? Once I'd had my ID photos taken and my timetable printed, I headed straight for the canteen. Fair enough, there were plenty of 'exciting' people milling around. Unfortunately, none of them seemed interested in meeting *me*.

Most people had been to the same feeder schools and I didn't have the balls to gatecrash those cosy cliques. Without the girls or Matt as backup, I was apparently a bit of a social doof. A crash course in gatecrashing, that's what I needed.

And the campus! Just leaving the foyer made my ears

pop and there was no chance I was *ever* finding my way round this mad maze of staircases, Hogwartsy nooks and crannies and never-ending corridors.

Confused, lost, overwhelmed, ignored . . . these emotions were definitely NOT mentioned in the brochure.

I clung to Rule #8 and tried thinking positive until break, when I wussed out and rang Ayesha.

'You've only been there for a couple of hours,' she said, when I'd unloaded my nearly-teary emotional splat. 'Stop skulking about like the ghost of no-mates past. Just walk up to someone and say hiya. Come on, what's the worst that could happen?'

'Well, the worst that could happen is they laugh in my face and the sound echoes through the whole building, attracting everyone's attention, and when they're all staring at me, my clothes mysteriously disappear meaning two thousand people see me naked and –'

'Enough!' she said.

'But what if you were right and I did rush into it? What if I should have stayed on at school?'

As the whine crept into my voice I swear I could *hear* her eyes rolling. 'Daisy, you have done NOTHING but slag St Mary's off all summer. The uniform. The teachers. The toilets. The dinners . . .'

'You hypocrite! Who started the petition to DNA-test "Mystery Meat" pie?'

'Yes, but we're not talking about me, are we? Oh. And the carpet tiles. You said they gave you static shocks.'

'They did!'

'Fine, but my point is you can't suddenly get nostalgic for school after a couple of hours at college. You need to give it more of a chance.'

Of course she was right. And anyway, school wouldn't be the same with Matt being in Spain. Us *not* getting the bus together. *Not* seeing him at break. *Not* sitting with him at dinner. Freaky-deaky. And that on top of everyone knowing he'd dumped me.

College hadn't ticked many boxes so far, but it certainly beat having my crappy-ever-after picked over by the gossip vultures.

'The bell's just rung,' Ayesha said. 'Look, me and Beth'd love you back here, but you need to give college a proper go before you think about jacking it in.'

I gave myself a mental arse-kicking there and then. *Think positive, Daisy:*

1. Induction day is a trailer, not the main event
2. There's no such thing as insta-mates
3. College will be what I make of it.

Now grow a pair and stop whingeing.

I'd been told to go to tutorial at eleven in room 71(b) so I walked back into the foyer to get my bearings just as the clock over the main entrance clicked to 10.56.

I had no idea where room 71(b) was. Four thousand (approx.) doors in the place, each numbered by a sadist with a black belt in sudoku. *Where is 71(b)? Upstairs? Uruguay? Uranus?* Despite Ayesha's best efforts to tame the panic demons, I couldn't help desperately missing my St Mary's-shaped comfort zone as I blundered up and down corridors that didn't lead to where I was supposed to be.

I was insanely flustered by the time I finally found the room. It was rammed to the ceiling tiles, meaning I had to squeeze through a tiny gap to get to an empty seat. And this was made infinitely worse because only ONE person (a Scarily Handsome Guy) stood up to let me pass.

I was rocking (Ayesha's carefully curated idea of) student style: Mum-made tea dress; vintage floral blazer (swirly shades of purple), plum tights and my trusty pink patent Doc Martens. Kooky cool. And, under the gaze of what felt like a million snidey eyeballs, I was nearly at my seat when this girl with an American twang went, 'Hey, why'd no one tell me it was fancy dress?'

Eh? Then the fake-baked twiglet cackled and my face flushed as pink as my boots at her smack-my-gob rudeness! And the *irony* because she was wearing the shortest, tightest, lowest garment imaginable: a neon orange dress so dazzlingly tacky it would have made my Nana Green wince and *she* had cataracts.

I was fluorescent with sweaty embarrassment myself by the time I finally sat down, thinking, *Did I miss the 'Meet snarky classmates' page in the prospectus?* At that precise moment I would've given my right arm with my vintage Biba bag slung over it to have Beth and Ayesha by my side.

Looked left: lad in a SpongeBob SquarePants T-shirt who smelled of rice cakes (or possibly wee), but at least he smiled in a friendly way. Then the teacher ('Call me Phil') came over and handed me a sticky address label, mouthing, 'Pop your name on that.'

I wrote *Daisy* with a little flower on the tail of the y, same as usual.

'*Okaaay*.' Call Me Phil perched on the edge of the desk, swinging his flip-flopped foot. 'As I was saying, you've all got a college email account and you should remember to check it every day. And now, here . . .' He chucked a beanbag at a lad in glasses. 'Tell the class your name plus three interesting facts about yourself. When you're done, pass it on. It's time for an ice-breaker methinks.'

Noooo! methought.

Every member of the class was eyeing the beanbag with horror. (Except the mouthy girl, who was almost exploding with *all about meeee!* ecstasy.)

The lad who'd caught the beanbag pushed his glasses up his nose. Not literally up his nostrils of course, because *that* would have been entertaining. No, instead he blinked a couple of times, then kicked off the I like football/pizza/telly/hate sprouts yawnathon which travelled round the room until it reached Scarily Handsome Guy, who practically had *What the actual f* . . . written across his perfect, modelsome features.

He picked the beanbag up carefully, taking his time, inspecting it. One side. The other. No rush. Then he pressed his hands on the desk and slowly levered himself to his feet.

It gave me a chance to get a better look at him. Tall, flawless, kind of Mediterranean-looking with his dark hair and olive complexion (as in tanned, not green or stuffed). From his sulky, fifties movie-icon expression to his very tight, very white T-shirt, he radiated this 'Look at me' subliminal command. An aura of awe. (An awe-ra?) Whatever it was, he turned fondling a manky beanbag into a mesmerising spectacle. The air zinged as we waited for him to speak and the bitchy American skankwomble began to drool.

'I'm Toby Smith,' Mr Incredible said eventually in a vaguely London accent. 'I'm seventeen and, sorry, I don't do ice-breakers.'

Then he slouched back down with professional-grade ennui and gently lobbed the beanbag at weedy SpongeBob who, judging by his face, urgently needed a clean pair of SquarePants. (And possibly a Sponge.)

'Er, h-h-hello everyone. Nice to meet you all. My name is Humphrey Badger and I-I . . .'

Well, coming after Toby King of Cool, the poor lad had no chance. The tension instantly shattered into yowls of 'Humphreeeeyyyyyyyy!'

'Quiet please!' Flip-flop Phil shouted. 'Enough, thank you, guys, shhhh.'

Humphrey raised his eyebrows along with his voice. 'So now you'll understand why I prefer to be called Badger. And yes, my parents do love me. And no, I'll never forgive them.' More laughs, kinder this time, and he gave the hint of a smile as the room quietened. 'OK, my three facts are: I've been home-schooled my whole life, I play the trumpet and the French horn, and I –'

But his last point was swallowed up by Miss Tanfastic screeching, '*French WHAT?!*' in a voice like nails scraping down an eardrum.

That did it. The room was in uproar again. I don't think anyone even noticed Badger sit down, cheeks flaming fifty shades of red as he slid the beanbag over to me.

Poor SpongeBob. My hands itched to deliver a little slap-justice on his behalf and I briefly daydreamed about running round the room, smacking every single guffawing goon across the chops.

This of course should've been Flip-flop Phil's job (maybe not the violence), but our tutor was being (in the immortal words of Nana Green) about as much use as an inflatable bloody dartboard. Flapping his arms, going, 'Hey . . . quiet now,' in an attempt to calm the cackles.

Yeah, like *that* was going to work.

With the beanbag in my hand and a blandly plastic smile on my face, I stood up as the howls faded to sniggers. Toby le Gorge was watching me, no trace of a smirk clouding those perfect features, but I hardly even noticed. I held out for pin-drop-level hush, then kept them waiting one beat, two beats, three beats more. Deep breath and:

'Hi everyone, my name's Daisy Green. My parents own a wedding business called Something Borrowed and I work part time for them. I love vintage clothes and playing football. And I absolutely, with a passion, *hate* bitchy people.' Then I chucked the beanbag, hard, at the girl in the neon, doll-sized dress. I'll give her this, she didn't bat an eyelid as she got to her feet.

'Thank you, Debbie. My name's Brittany Bentley and three amazing facts about me are: my mom's from England, but I grew up in Texas. I'm a cheerleader and my team made it to nationals in Atlanta this spring, which was awesome; I love competitive dancing, especially disco and Latin; I got into the televised rounds of *America's Got Talent* last year and I want to be . . . famous!'

As she flashed a creepy pageant-princess smile, my

immediate thoughts were: a) *That's not three things* and b) *Who the hell is Debbie?*

No one else seemed to notice though, and loads of the boys started wolf whistling and *awwwoooo*-ing. (Toby and Badger-not-Humphrey earned instant brownie points for their non-joining in.) Brittany flicky-flicked her hair and did a fake *aw shucks* curtsy.

Famous? Yawn. Way to go, Stereotype Girl.

Me and Badger smiled at each other.

'Daisy, yeah?' he whispered, holding out his hand. 'As in flower?'

'Badger, yeah?' I replied, shaking it. 'As in vicious, striped woodland creature?'

'Erm, yes. Hello.'

'Hi.'

'Did you hear the one about the beanbag?' he said.

'No?'

'It didn't break the ice.'

Arf arf. Lame cracker jokes aside, at least he was friendly, which instantly catapulted him above the rest of the people I'd met so far. Then he said bye he had to rush off to music, and I got my timetable out. Now, where was D Block?

By the time I'd worked out I was already in D Block

(duh), the room was empty except for Scarily Handsome Toby. Odd. I glanced around, expecting to see a crowd of his mates lurking somewhere, but no. He was waiting for *me*.

His sulk-face had been erased by a smile so hot it probably had the power to vaporise knickers (Other girls' knickers anyway. Mine were 100 per cent smile-proof thanks to Matt.) 'Are you on a free now?' he asked.

'No, I'm just late for next lesson,' I said. 'Got my Spanish induction.'

'No worries,' he said with a wink, an action that would normally set me cringing for England. Except from him it weirdly kind of didn't. 'I'll see you later then, Daisy.'

'Yeah, bye,' I said, smiling.

Nice guy. Cute. It almost made up for catty Brittany. *Almost*.

And I suppose the rest of the day wasn't that bad, not burning-in-the-sulphurous-pits-of-Hell bad anyway. More un-good, like finding an umbrella in your Christmas stocking: hardly *Yay, gift of my dreams*, but not quite *Kill me now* territory either.

I guess the biggest shock was how similar college was to school. Maybe there were no bells, no uniform, no registration. (No friends . . . sigh.) But from the *Dirty Porridge* painted walls, to the perma-reek of Lynx and chips, I could have been back at St Mary's.

The Rule #8 Think Positive List
Here, I could be Just Daisy not
DaisywhogotdumpedbyMatt.
The toilets were clean.
No uniform.
OK-ish teachers.

It wasn't a mistake. Right?
Right?!
And speaking of mistakes, Brittany must've though it was fancy dress herself. I mean, why else would anyone walk round dressed as a Bratz doll?

After college, I caught the bus to footie training and then me and Ayesha went back to hers.

'How was school?' I said as I sat down on her bed. 'Everyone missing me already?'

'Well, me and Beth certainly are,' she answered. 'And Mr Fox asked after you in registration.'

'Old Captain Comb-over? Really?'

Given our years of mutual loathing in form time and maths I was stunned he didn't get the party poppers out when I failed my GCSE. Or fall to his knees and weep with joy when I told him I wasn't coming back.

'Shocker, I know. He said to give you his best wishes for college.'

Blimey.

'And I think he really meant it.'

Double blimey with sprinkles on top. He must have been wetting his flares in case I changed my mind about leaving.

I opened my mouth, ready to cast a *think positive* spin on my day when the doorbell rang. It was Beth. Apparently she wasn't grounded as long as she agreed to her dad following her wherever she went. As in *he was sitting outside in the car.* Beyond creepy.

However, my initial mad-dad sympathy soon drained away as the endless tears Beth snotted down Ayesha's cardigan turned my heart to stone. And after five minutes of her, *But I loooove Shaneeey*, driving me up the Wailing Wall, I could not hold my tongue another second.

'Don't take this the wrong way, but maybe your dad's got a point.'

Beth's head popped up, a mascara-smeared meerkat

sensing danger. 'What do you mean?'

'Maybe it's time you tried being single for a bit.'

'Single? What the hell for?' She sounded genuinely surprised.

'Oh God, I don't know. Because you've never tried it? Because you're making yet another mistake?'

'What mistake?'

'I mean . . .' I breathed in deep. 'From what I've heard, I don't think this Shaney is good news.'

'Oh yeah?' she said, folding her arms and giving me the bring-it-on eyes. 'Why not?'

'Well, for starters, he followed you home from school.'

'Only to talk!'

I rolled my eyes. 'Talk . . . stalk . . .'

'Daisy . . .' said Ayesha in a warning tone.

'I'm staging a Rule number 5 intervention,' I said defensively. '*Always be honest . . .*'

'. . . *even when it's painful*,' Ayesha finished. 'I know, I know. But I don't think now is the right time.' She gave an exaggerated nod in Beth's direction and grimaced.

'Well, excuse *me*,' interrupted Beth, with a Jeremy Kyle guest hand/head shake 'n' wag. 'It's up to me who I go out with, not you. Stop interfering.'

This was the exact moment at which an emergency gob-stop would have been advisable. Sadly, it appeared my mouth had missed the memo.

'It's not *me* who's interfering with you, is it?' I said.

'*Daisy!*' said Ayesha, more urgently this time.

I rolled my eyes heavenwards again. 'For God's sake, Beth, get real; he's a complete pervatron.'

'You've never even met him,' she snapped. 'You don't know anything about him.'

'I know he's a bouncer with a misspelled neck tattoo who follows schoolgirls home.'

'I love him!'

'And I love animals,' I said, 'but I wouldn't particularly want to start a relationship with one.'

Beth glared, presumably aiming for haughty, but too red-faced and snot-encrusted to carry it off. Ayesha inhaled, poised to rub some verbal Savlon on our bitch scratches, but before she got a word out, Lady Boohoo took a final swipe.

'You're jealous, Daisy, that's your problem. Bitter and heartless and jealous. The only reason you want me single is so you won't be the only one without a boyfriend. Because since Matt left you can't stand to see anyone happy.'

Ouch. That hurt so much.

I didn't even stay to state the obvious, *Er, who's happy?* I just grabbed my coat and stormed past Ayesha's lovely mum in the hall and Beth's bonkers dad on the street.

But as I walked home, muttering, 'Bitter, am I? Jealous?' under my breath, my anger began to recede. Had I been too harsh? *Was* I really being the Queen of Stony Hearts?

It was true that Matt broke my heart when he went to Spain. (And by 'broke' I mean 'tore out and pounded to lifeless, smushy goop'.) But that didn't mean I wanted everyone else to be miserable too. Especially not my friends.

But get real! Any primary schoolkid could have told Beth that if a strange man followed you home, you should report him to the police, not hand him your phone number. No exceptions. And to call it love, *puh-lease*. She barely knew him.

Beth was a first-class drama farmer. Every other week she created some new boyfriend crisis and expected me and Ayesha to just jump on the emoto-cycle with her.

Phase 1. Ignore the warning signs.

Phase 2. Expect Daisy and Ayesha to pick up the pieces.

Rinse and repeat.

Well, I'd had it with her Goddess of Melodrama act. Maybe you couldn't judge a book by its cover, but I was pretty sure you could spot a twat by his tatts.

She needed to take those wanker blinkers off once and for all and it was my and Ayesha's duty to remind her of the Never-to-be-Broken #1 Golden Rule for Girls: *It is* always *better to be single than to date a twat.*

CHAPTER 4

AAAARGH. Forget Stony Hearts, I was the medal-winning, record-breaking Queen Gormless of Twatania. Never, in the history of womankind, had anyone ever shown less gorm or more twat (figuratively speaking) than I did the second time I spoke to Toby.

I'd bumped into Badger a couple of times since Monday's induction tutorial, but even though I'd kept a tiny eye out for Toby, our paths hadn't crossed again. Until now.

I was sitting in the library, headphones on, and completely engrossed in *Wuthering Heights* when *swisssh:* an unidentified yellow object sailed over my head and landed *thud* on the desk.

Turn: no one there.

What the . . .?

Back to desk: bag of sweets.

Turn again: still no one.

Back to desk: *mmmmm*, Jelly Babies. *Nom nom*.

Weird. I picked up my book and was back roaming the moors with grumpy old Heathcliff when I sensed a Scarily Handsome Presence.

My eyes travelled up slowly. Hipster trainers, pair of jeans, tight white T-shirt, moody movie-star face, mop of black hair. *Down a bit*. Smile so pretty it made me want to cry.

'Hi, I'm Toby. We're in form together. Daisy, isn't it?'

'Er, yes, that's right. Hello.'

He gestured at the Jelly Babies. 'You looked in need of cheering up. Sorry if I made you jump.'

In Fantasyland, where I wasn't a tit with the social skills of a four-year-old, we would have chatted like two normal people. HOWEVER, because I am the Queen of Twatania, what actually happened was this:

Me: 'Er, it's OK. Thanks.'

Toby: (*pointing at Jelly Babies*) I bite their heads off first.

Me: 'I'm a bottom-biter myself.' (*casually pick up Jelly Baby; completely miss mouth; scrabble on floor*)

Toby: (*pause*) '*Okaaaay*, well, enjoy your book. See you later.'

Me: (*cringe cringe, stuff whole fist in mouth, CRINGE*) 'See you.'

Aaaargh. Toby Smith was not just potential friend material, Toby Smith was potential friend material coated in a sumptuous layer of incredible and dusted with jaw-dropping perfection. And what did I do? Self-lobotomise.

Bottom-biter.

Sometimes I really *really* hated myself.

Anyway, I went round to Ayesha's after college again. Partly to make sure the two of us were OK post-Shaneygate Beth bust-up, but mainly to reassure myself I was only a friend-free loser between the hours of nine and four. Cringer-sation with the Divine Toby aside, I didn't speak to a single fellow student all day.

On the bus, I ummed and ahhed before deciding not to tell her about the Jelly Baby episode because a) it would mean confessing to my bottom-biting idiocy, b) she'd get giddy over what was, essentially, a non-event and c) we only had half an hour before she went to her boyfriend Tom's to play with his telescope. (Not a euphemism.)

'Why don't you come too? There's a spectacular meteor shower forecast and if the cloud holds off it should be properly dramatic.'

This was said with the enthusiasm most teens reserve for the phrases 'parents going away' and 'house party'. Bless her geeky little heart. But I had to get home to babysit River while Mum and Dad picked up the tablecloths for Saturday from the hire place.

That was the thing with running a wedding business: people assumed it was a once a week in the summer kind of job. No chance. Something Borrowed was flat out year round. When they weren't collecting supplies, Mum was sorting the playlist or rehearsing with Uncle Harvey's band, Something Blue, fitting a gown, creating table decorations, checking venues, visiting vintage fairs or any of a billion other things she could turn her multitalented hands to. And if Dad wasn't photographing a bride and groom, he was busy baking and sculpting the most incredible wedding cakes this side of, well, anywhere. I helped out by doing lot of babysitting. And eating *a lot* of cake.

'Sorry, I can't tonight,' I said. 'But I am going to ring Beth to clear the air.'

Ayesha pulled her *hmmmm* face. 'I'd better warn you: she has not stopped going on today about what you said about Shaney. You really pissed her off.'

'Well, one of us needs to give her some tough love,' I said. 'If we both go "yeah, great" every time she lands another slack-ass, she'll keep on till she's pulling pensioners. We can't lie just to make her feel better.'

'Beth doesn't think Shaney is a slack-ass though, does she? Quite the contraire, she actually thinks she's found the man of her dreams.' Ayesha put her hands on her hips, signalling the conversation was entering the bossy phase. 'This means we, or more specifically *you*, need to start being more supportive and stop being mean about a guy you haven't even met.'

'Pah. If Shaney's the man of her dreams, she's set the bar so low it's lying on the floor,' I snorted. 'No, in fact, the bar is actually *subterranean*.'

Before Ayesha had a chance to respond, her mum rapped once on the door then walked in, looking remarkably glamorous for a woman who'd spent her day chopping bunions, it has to be said. Not an orthopaedic clog/nylon tunic in sight.

'You look amazing, Mrs Stokes,' I whistled. 'I love that dress.' Fit and flare black cat-print midi with one net underskirt by the look of it.

She grinned and did a twirl. 'Thanks.'

'Guess who's going on a *date*,' said Ayesha, putting an arm round her mum.

'It's just a cup of coffee,' she said, squeezing Ayesha into a quick hug. 'I'll only be an hour or so.'

'Have fun!' me and Ayesha chorused.

'Will do!' she shouted from the stairs.

'Date, eh?' I said when the front door had closed. 'How do you feel about that, you know, after what happened last time?'

Ayesha sat back on the bed. 'I think it's great she's finally ready to get out there again.'

'Has she heard from Dan at all?'

'No, but that hasn't stopped her stressing.' Ayesha frowned, twisting the corner of the duvet in her hands. 'Not just about herself either. She worries about him doing the same to someone else.'

'Isn't he on some kind of *avoid this man* register?'

Ayesha shrugged. 'Not sure there is one.'

Of course not. Go too fast, get banned from driving. Shoplift, get banned from town. Beat a dog, get banned from owning animals. Abuse your partner, get a lifetime relationship ban? Er, no.

So what was in place to stop He-devil Dan torturing the next woman unlucky enough to fall for him? Big fat zilch and zero, apparently.

'A date's a good sign though,' I said, keeping my grim thoughts to myself. 'First step type thing.'

'Yeah,' she smiled. 'This guy works with her cousin. She only went cos he came with a personal recommendation. No way she'll go internet man-shopping again.'

'References,' I agreed. 'I get that. No more nasty surprises.'

Of course, the real nasty surprise was that Dan had stayed Big Bad News for so long. Even though it had been over a year since they'd split, those few months had cast a massive shadow.

I think what made it more of a shock was Ayesha's mum being pretty much the last person you'd picture with an utter nutter. But I guess control freaks don't advertise. *Hi, I'm Dan, six feet two with eyes of blue. I like long walks on the beach, Thai green curry and terrorising women.*

That's what I've learned. Doesn't matter what age, gender, IQ, personality – there is no such thing as a typical situation. If it could happen to someone like Ayesha's mum, it could happen to anyone.

Which made Ayesha's fence-sitting over Beth even more mystifying because if ever a man had a neon arrow over his head flashing AVOID AVOID AVOID it was Shaney, and yet she was telling me to be 'more understanding'. I didn't get it.

On the walk home I rang Beth once, twice, three times with no answer. This suggested she was either de-grounded and out with her badly inked boy (unlikely) or in a humungous strop with me. Either way it didn't matter. I knew as soon as Shaney joined Stinky Pete and Co. on the scrapheap, she'd be phoning me to say I'd been right all along.

Mum was pulling on her boots in the hall as I let myself in.

'River's had his bath and he's just got into bed. Me and Dad should be back around nine.' She picked up her coat. 'Thanks for doing this, love.'

I crept upstairs and, after removing a fluffy *T-rex*, perched on the edge of River's bed. I was tucking the duvet round his shoulders when he spoke, his voice slightly muffled, but the words clear. 'Daisy, when is Matt coming back?'

Ouch. It totally killed me that River missed Matt nearly as much as I did. If my heart wasn't already broken, his sad little voice would've cracked it in two. 'I don't know, little man,' I said steadily. 'Now why don't I read you a story?'

It took several Gruffaloes and a Mr Tickle before he finally dropped off, Biohazard (aka Teddy) clutched in his arms. And as he drifted off to the Land of Nod, I drifted off to the sofa, planning a trash telly fest. But when I flicked through the property/cookery/travel show old-fartathon specials, I just couldn't concentrate.

In search of more effective distraction, I headed up to my room. If the real world held nothing of interest, maybe the virtual one would. I unearthed my pile o'crap laptop from under the pile o'crap on my desk.

Pressed the button. Waited. Tidied the top layer of my desk. Waited some more. Aeons passed; dynasties crumbled; civilisations rose and fell before my home page shuddered to life. But even then leafing through other people's happy updates and smiley photos did nothing to lift my mood.

I suddenly felt very, very fed up.

Fed up of wishing Matt's mum hadn't watched so many travel programmes. Fed up of pretending to be OK. Fed up of waiting to feel happy again.

Mainly, though, I was just fed up of being fed up.

There was nothing but spam in my home email and

I was expecting the same of my college one when, as Flip-flop Phil had instructed, I logged in.

And got the surprise of my life.

Hidden deep among the dreary admin-crap was a shiny and unexpected gem:

Subject: Stranger Danger
Daisy,
Didn't your parents teach you not to take sweets from strangers?
Toby x

Eh? In some dusty corner of Heartbreak Hell, a drowsy memory opened one eye. God, what was it called again? That thing when someone waited for you after a lesson, gave you sweets, sent an email . . . Tip of my tongue . . . Fl-? Fli-? Flir-?

Dun dun durrr! Was Toby Smith *flirting* with me?

Wow. I sat back in my desk chair and reread the words on the screen, trying to assess the angle of his dangle: was it frisky or friendly? Impossible to tell.

What I needed was a response that walked the tricky tightrope between frosty and fangirl. A witty, effortless email that made it clear I was off limits without sounding like a bitch, basically.

Easy, right?

Ha ha. I could've learned to write Japanese quicker.

Subject: Re: Stranger Danger
Toby,
We'd already met, so technically you weren't a
stranger and Jelly Babies aren't dangerous anyway.
(Except when you bite their bottoms).
Thank you though, they did cheer me up.
Daisy x

I agonised over the words and then over the kiss.
Trialled a version with it in, a version with it out. Kissy
hokey-cokey. Still, that little flirty email arrived just in
the nick of time to resuscitate my dying self-esteem.

I smiled. Perhaps college wouldn't be a disaster
after all.

CHAPTER 5

The next day, I sat next to Badger in form. I still hadn't quite figured him out. Like, was he a bit *Curious Incident* or plain old-school geek? He was wearing a *Lion King* T-shirt, which might have been an ironic statement, and playing the trumpet was pretty cool. But he did smell a tiny bit of wee (or possibly rice cakes) so it was hard to be sure.

Not that it mattered. *Takes all sorts to make a world* as Nana Green always said.

Badger smiled and I opened my mouth, but before a word could come out, Toby 'stranger danger' Smith strutted in and sent my mind AWOL.

Shame on me for having the heart of a weak and feeble muppet, but I'd had a 'ho hum' moment when my inbox told me 'no new messages'. Only a fleeting one though, before I pulled my emotional socks up and refused to give in to disappointment.

Did you learn nothing from Matt the Rat, Daisy Green? No reply, no big deal. Remember: think positive.

Or at least that was the theory. I spent breakfast and the bus journey so-what-ing myself up to the max . . . and then he walked in and my heart skipped a beat. Curse you, traitorous internal organ.

Brittany was *veeery* attentive as Toby and his movie-star aura strolled across the room. Until he sat in the chair next to me, that is, then she glowered like I'd just thrown up in her handbag. *Ha ha and booooya, Bratzilla!*

All eight foot whatever of Toby was radiating this *Look at me, look at meeee* magnetic pull on my eyeballs, and if the tattered remnants of my heart didn't still belong to Matt, I would definitely have been tempted.

Jeez, he was so gorgeous it was unreal, like a Greek god in a hoodie. He winked (endearingly) and a daft grin blossomed on my face.

Toby: 'Morning, Daisy. Did you sleep well?'

(Subtext: *Bet you were up all night checking your emails*.)

Me: 'I slept like a baby, thanks.'

(Subtext: *Don't flatter yourself, matey*.)

He smirked.

(Subtext: *Touché*)

So things were looking up. Until Phil flip-flopped in anyway.

'*Okaaaay*,' he said. 'Today we're going to spend some time learning more about each other and, consequently, more about ourselves.'

Daft grin gone. Oh please, Lord, no more beanbags.

'And for this one I need you all to get in pairs, so if you could sort that now, please.'

Toby and Badger spoke simultaneously. 'Daisy —'

Awkward.

'Sorry, mate. Maybe next time,' Toby said, and much as I was starting to like him, it instantly triggered the underdog sirens in my head.

'Actually,' I shifted my bag slightly along the desk, 'I'm going to work with Badger.'

Smiling, Toby said, 'No problem,' to me then called out, 'Hey, Brittany? You in a pair?'

'I could be,' she said, licking her lips.

'Come here then.' He screeched his chair along to create a space while she almost gave herself whiplash in her haste to comply.

God, she was so obvious. And Toby too. Clearly, he was one of those very good-looking lads who thought he could click his fingers and girls' pants would fall to the floor.

Well not this girl.

And definitely not these pants.

Badger had his friendly Labrador grin on when I turned back round. Bless him.

'Rice cake?' He pulled a *Star Wars* lunch box out of his rucksack.

'Not for me, thanks,' I said, smiling and taking a worksheet from Phil.

'*Okaaay*, you guys,' he said as he perched on the desk. 'Excitement and personal growth await each and every one of us. Join me as we venture forth, united in our incredible voyage of self-discovery. Together, we will sail on the seas of wonder and land on the shores of empowerment. Destination: the very core of our inner selves and some truly astonishing revelations.' Flip-flops a gogo, he gazed around the room. Then he coughed. 'Now, does anyone need to borrow a pencil?'

Blah.

After that build-up, I wanted my mind well and truly blown. But no. Some utterly lame-o activities to uncover our learning styles commenced. *Trees died for THIS?* I thought.

Badger started trawling through the tedious questionnaire, frowning and scribbling notes, while I discreetly eavesdropped on the flirty banter (flanter?) drifting over from my left. Now that *was* what you'd call revealing.

Toby and Brittany filled in the worksheet, laughing and joking, heads bowed closely together . . . EXCEPT (and this was definitely not my imagination) as she threw herself into fangirling hyperdrive, he was glancing sideways at me and Badger, as if keeping tabs on what I was doing. Which naturally, because I was a professional Icicle Knickers, was 100 per cent NOT horizontally eyeballing him back.

Questionnaires completed, we had a class feedback sesh (during which it transpired we each learned best by reading, listening and doing. Wowsers.) and it was the end of the lesson.

Badger had music, I was hanging about till maths and Brittany presumably had plans to continue flirting her lady lumps off, judging by the way she was panting over Toby. When we got to the door, Toby paused to let her out first and she brushed past with a girly tee-hee-hee. Then he turned to look directly at me and raised one eyebrow.

Now, I don't speak eyebrow, but if I had to take a

punt I'd guess it meant, *What is she like?*

I was still processing this as he followed Brittany out.

Got home from college to find Mum on the phone with Mrs Boyle, being told some un-be-flaming-lievable news: Beth had only gone and moved in with Shaney!

From my listening post on the stairs, I learned Beth had had an apocalyptic row with her warden (sorry, *dad*) after he insisted on picking her up from school and locking her in her cell (sorry, *room*). But Beth climbed out of the window when they were watching telly. (Not that impressive: she lives in a bungalow.)

In the morning, when he realised she'd gone, Mr B had driven straight to the police station demanding Shaney's arrest for molesting his daughter, but because Beth is over sixteen they told him it was a 'domestic matter'. Meaning technically she could have shacked up at the Playboy mansion if she'd fancied it. (*Erk.*)

With no help from the law, Mr Boyle set off to The Rat and Drainpipe to 'teach that cradle-snatching scrote a lesson he'll never forget'. Which, considering Shaney was Bob the Bodybuilder and Mr B put the wet in lettuce, was unlikely. But Shaney wasn't working there any more.

Bloody hell though, what was she thinking? Love

might be blind, but apparently in Beth's case it was also deaf and very, very dumb.

I checked my emails on the off chance, but there was nothing else interesting on the college system. My home inbox, however, had a new message from Matt. Just seeing his name was like a smack in the face.

I never told anyone this, but in a moment of utter spinelessness one sad night about a week after he left, I sent Matt a long, long email.

In it I said how I regretted that stupid ultimatum and that I missed him to the point of physical pain. How I couldn't face going back to St Mary's without him. How, right up till the moment he got on the plane, I never believed he'd go through with it.

I virtually scraped my heart out and splattered it across the screen *begging* him to come back to England.

And he said no.

Of course, he said it in a lovely way, how it wasn't forever, but he still said he wasn't coming home. That's when I decided the whole 'let's be friends' thing wasn't for me.

So, whatever he had to tell me now, I didn't want to hear it.

I hit delete.

CHAPTER 6

Next morning I didn't feel much more cheerful as I heaved my lazy carcass out of bed at far too early o'clock for brekkie, bathroom, bus. Matt's absence was providing the usual downbeat backing track to my daily routine, but the email had turned the volume up. Texted Beth to check she was OK (no reply) and there it was: another crap day had begun.

Or so I thought.

Walking through reception, I felt a random tap on my shoulder. When I'd peeled myself off the ceiling tiles, I took my headphones out and turned round.

'Sorry,' the tapper said. 'Didn't mean to make you jump. You OK?'

'Er, yes thanks, Toby. You?'

He yawned. 'Yeah, not bad. Got some IT homework to

do, but I'm not in the zone. What time's your first class?'

'Ten, but my bus always gets in for nine.'

'Come for a drink with me?'

And there it was: a coffee with Toby. An event registering an impressive eight on the what-the-heckograph. Not because I felt unworthy of his attention. To use a housing metaphor, I considered myself 'prime real estate', highly desirable to the right buyer. But while I was a quirky holiday cottage with honeysuckle round the door, he was Mr Loft in Manhattan. Slate and steel.

In other words, we weren't exactly matchmadeinheaven.com.

But what harm could a brew do? 'Sure,' I replied, automatically turning canteenwards.

'Not here,' he said, steering me towards the exit. 'I've got a car. Let's go somewhere decent.'

Without even a fleeting flash of stranger danger I followed him to where, hidden among the teachers' knackered heaps, was his freshly minted mini convertible. A gleaming black diamond in a scrapyard.

'Nice car,' I said imaginatively.

'Present from my mum,' he said. 'You OK with The Mean Bean?'

I nodded, put my seat belt on and, roof down in the

almost sunshine, we sped out of the college grounds. Just like that. One minute, I was Nelly No-mates on a bus that smelled of socks; the next, in a flash car with a man so perfect he probably sweated aftershave.

Oh, how the other half lives, I thought.

'Skinny latte and an Americano. Black.' Boy Gorgeous told the barista five minutes later, then turned to me. 'Skinny OK?'

'Er, yes, that's fine,' I answered, although truthfully I was craving hot chocolate with extra whipped cream and a marshmallow mountain of Everest proportions.

'Nothing to eat, no?'

'Er, no thanks.'

He ordered himself a croissant and we sat down on a squashy corner sofa.

'Do you fancy a nibble?' he said with a cheeky eyebrow flex.

The born-again Icicle Knickerist in me smiled back. 'Not hungry, thanks.'

It was strange. I could flirt with aplomb when I had a boyfriend. Suddenly single and bang, my aplomb was gone.

A couple of tables down, a group of girls a bit older than us were peering over the rims of their mugs.

Obviously it wasn't li'l ol' me they were ogling, but Toby didn't even seem to notice. Instead, he leaned forward to spoon a pile of sugar into his mug. Wow. So fit, he'd developed an immunity to being leched at. He was perv-resistant.

'So,' I said, 'how you finding college?'

'OK, I guess. It's my second time round though. Dropped out last year.' He looked at me. 'Long story.'

'Where were you before?'

He stirred the coffee slowly. 'Down south. How about you?'

'College? Not what I was expecting.' I shrugged.

'What were you expecting?'

I took a sip of my latte and grew a sexy foam tache. Nice. 'I dunno, different from school, I suppose. Maybe the people to be more . . .'

'Studenty?'

'Yeah, I guess. Less cliquey maybe. Or at least less like Brit–' I stopped mid-name, remembering their chummy chatting in form yesterday.

'Brittany? Dumb slut,' he said, casually dunking a piece of croissant.

Whatever the opposite of a poker face is called, I must've pulled one. I hated that word, just hated it, no matter who it was applied to. OK, so I wouldn't be waving my cheerleader's pompoms for Brittany Bentley any time soon, but throwing an S-grenade at her?

Toby must've guessed exactly what I was thinking. He back-pedalled so fast, his tongue practically started spinning.

'Oops, that came out harsher than I intended. But she was a bitch for laughing at you and that weird kid, whatshisname, Bodger?'

'Badger.'

'Yeah, yeah. Him. I mean, he can't help being a geek, can he?'

I was losing the thread here. Was he being kind about Badger? Mean about Brittany? Did he slip in a compliment about me somewhere?

Meanwhile, the girls at the other table were now indulging in some blatant gawpage. Brazen. So very rude, in fact, that if I was his girlfriend, I'd've gone a whole bunch of bananas over it.

I was on extremely unfamiliar ground here; strangers never openly *phwoooa*red at Matt when we were out together. Not that he needed a paper bag over his head in public or anything, but he was no lady dazzler. Unlike Toby.

'So, you're from down south?' I asked.

'Yep.'

'Have you still got family there?'

'What's this? An interrogation?' He sat back in his chair and cracked his knuckles.

'Erm, no, just asking.'

Like flicking a switch, he grinned again. 'Only kidding. Yes, some. Near London. We moved up here at the beginning of last year.'

'And where are you living now?' I said it hesitantly.

'Near college.'

'With your mum and dad?'

'Mum and her boyfriend.'

Flip. His smile vanished before the question was out of my mouth. I was sensing mucho history behind those not-elaborating vibes. Toby continued sipping his coffee in silence as an awkward pause hopped up on to my chair to join us.

'But that's enough about me,' he said after what felt like a decade. 'Tell me about you.'

That did it. Tongue untied, my mouth jumped at the invitation. Oh ye gods of soul-curling embarrassment, how I talked over the next twenty minutes. And talked. And talked. Something Borrowed and the weddings. Mum singing with Something Blue. Dad's photography and cakes. River. Ayesha and Tom. Beth and Shaney. Even old Mr Fox got a mention.

Did Toby need to know I once got a dried chickpea stuck up my nose? That I was borderline phobic about Babybels ('It's the way they squeak!')? That I was conceived on (or possibly under) a pile of coats?

NO!

What was I thinking? I'd managed to turn a perfectly innocent hot-beverage break into a confessional cringeathon. Even putting my pillow over my head and screaming *aaaargh* wouldn't end the unbearable humiliation. (Trust me, I tried.)

One, two, three . . . take a deep breath.

Open eyes.

Unclench entire body.

Aaaand relax.

Matt was easier to read than a Mr Men book, but Toby . . . When I was nervous, I could talk the hind leg off a *Gigantosaurus*. A whole herd of them in fact. Sentences waffled out of my mouth while I listened, helplessly.

I learned Toby once lived near London. He got *The Complete Works of Daisy Green*, every detail minus pin number, bra size and . . .

'Boyfriend?'

I shook my head. 'We broke up in June.'

'Sorry to hear that.'

'It's all right.' I shrugged slightly. 'You know, it wasn't great at the time but . . .'

Then it was my turn to give off the *I don't wanna talk about it* vibes. Toby just carried on watching me as I peeped back under lowered eyelids, his very obvious scrutiny making me a nervy jumble of thrilled and on edge. Then he shifted us on to neutral ground and, by the time I'd reached the dregs of my coffee, we'd traded comedy box set quotes and discovered a shared infatuation with nineties indie rock and horror flicks.

First impressions? There was a quality to him that I couldn't put my finger on. Yes, his handsomeness flew off the scale. Yes, he'd be a dead cert for gold in the Charm Olympics. But there was something else, this Tobyness, as if he lived more intensely in the moment. Like the whole time I was wittering my nonsense, he never once took his eyes away; I don't think he even blinked.

Then, because time certainly flies when you're a burbling, bean-spilling fool, it was nearly ten and our cue to rush back to college. And as Toby strode to the café exit, the gawping girls turned their heads in a synchronised wave of *phwoooar*.

We made it back to the foyer with literally seconds for me to get up four flights of stairs. Quick bye-thanks-for-the-coffee, and I turned to go, but he caught my arm.

'I'm not sorry," he said.

My face must have replied, 'confused'.

'I mean I'm not sorry you split up with your boyfriend.'

Then he vanished into the throng.

I sprinted to Spanish where I swear I tried to focus on the pluperfect-whatevers, but my concentration was fried.

Not entirely sure how it happened, but it appeared I'd gained a head-squatter. Somehow, despite my Icicle Knicker intentions, Toby had wormed his way into my subconscious and was holding my brain hostage.

Luckily Ayesha came round after school for me to do her nails and I knew I could rely on her to give me some good advice of the *Forget the guy. He sounds like a player. You need some single-girl recovery time* variety.

Two coats of *Freshly Bleeding Corpse* later and she was up to speed with events at The Mean Bean. Finally, I'd have the words to evict Toby from my head.

Or not . . .

'It might do you good, you know, having a flirt buddy. Stop you pining over Matt.'

What? 'I am not pining over him! In fact, I –'

'Daisy, you're not fooling anyone, least of all me.' Her words cut my denialogue off at the knees. 'Say Tom was Matt, I wouldn't be embarrassed to show my feelings because it's normal to be upset when you break up with someone, especially after three years. Remember Beth with whatshisname?'

'Stinky Pete?' I said. She shook her head. 'Mad Max?' I went on, 'Manhobbit?' *Shake.* 'Not-Very-Big Ben? Wonky –'

'Will,' she finished triumphantly, nodding. 'Wonky Will, that's it. She was in bits and that only lasted four weeks. I guess what I'm saying is, you don't have to act as if it's no big deal when it bloody is. There are no medals for being brave, you know.'

'Yes there are.'

'You know what I mean. Outside wartime.'

'But Toby never asked me on a date or anything. You're getting all "flirt buddy" over nothing.'

She blew on her newly crimsoned fingertips then waggled them in my face. 'Daisy, listen to your Auntie Ayesha. If it looks like a duck and it quacks like a duck, chances are it's not a giraffe.'

'Eh?'

'I mean, numbskull, that this morning was a date. He didn't need to ask you out because you were already out.'

'Going for coffee in college time is not a date,' I insisted.

She tutted, exasperated. 'If you say so. How'd you get talking to him anyway?'

'Tutorial. Then he threw some Jelly Babies at me.'

She looked smug. 'See? Lads don't do stuff like that if they're not interested. Honestly, I think you should go for it.'

The conversation was veering completely off-script here.

'I don't need a boyfriend, thanks,' I told her.

'No one *needs* a boyfriend,' said Ayesha. 'Like no one *needs* chocolate fudge cake or vintage handbags or . . .' She looked round my room, ending on my pillow. 'A Hello Kitty pyjama case.'

'Matt bought me that,' I protested, hugging it tightly to my chest. 'It's got sentimental value.'

'Exactly. You don't *need* it, but you like it and having it around sparklifies your life.'

'Is that even a word?'

'I'm not saying you have to marry this Toby guy,' she continued, 'but I don't think one date would be a bad idea.'

I smoothed the pyjama case and placed it carefully back on my pillow. 'You're getting way ahead of yourself; he hasn't even asked for my phone number.'

She smirked. '*Yet*. Bet you anything he asks you out properly before the weekend.'

'Ayesha,' I said, sarcastically, 'you are wiser than the owl offspring of Yoda and the Dalai Lama. You are sager than –'

'Shut up!' she said and threw the pyjama case at me.

Now I knew she meant well, but no way was I ready for dating again.

Meaning that even though Toby Smith had the OMG-factor; even though he was Prince Fittie of Fitlandia and even though he had charmed the Icicle Knickers right off me that morning, it was irrelevant.

This little piggy was OFF the market.

After Ayesha left, I went with Dad and River to Something Blue's rehearsal for the wedding gig on Saturday. Firmly pushing away the thought that I'd (possibly) been conceived on top of his coat, (eew) I greeted my godfather Harvey with a kiss on the cheek while Marvin, his husband, gave us a cheery wave from behind the drum kit.

Then one, two, three, he counted them in and *wow*.

Yes, of course I was biased, but when Mum sang she could put a new spin on love songs you'd heard a million times. And the sweetest thing was every word was sung for Dad.

Aww.

Forget dragons and castles and knights on white horses and all that fairy-tale balls. *This* was true love. OK, maybe most sixteen-year-olds wouldn't want to follow in their parents' romantic footsteps, but I did. Their once-in-a-lifetime love was what I thought I'd found with Matt.

Even after seventeen years together, Dad's default expression was, *I can't believe my luck*. Mum's was, *Me neither*.

Thanks to Matt the Rat, mine went, *How did I get it so wrong?*

Anyway, me, Dad and River started clapping as the last note faded, but Harv was frowning. He unhooked his guitar strap and turned to face Mum and Marv, who was tapping the air absent-mindedly with his drumsticks.

'You know guys, it's dog eat dog out there and while the Something Blue sound is tight, we need to keep pushing the musical envelope. We need a USP.'

'A what?' asked Mum and Marv together.

'Unique Selling Point,' Harv said thoughtfully. 'Ukulele, banjo, slide trombone. Brass, strings . . . whatever. An edge. The question is, do we know anyone who's available?'

Badger's ice-breaker. 'I met a lad at college who plays the trumpet,' I long-shotted into the ensuing silence. 'And the French horn.'

'Trumpet,' echoed Harv. He and Marv chin-stroked in unison. 'They're versatile creatures, horn players. Good presence. A good horn owns the stage. Invite him for a jam, yeah?'

'Sure,' I said, regretting the words as soon as they were out because:

a) Badger's playing may suck for all I knew.
b) 'Presence?' The guy got upstaged by a beanbag.

Rehearsal over, we'd hardly got in through the front door before Mrs Boyle rang again with an update. Beth had said she'd only come home if her parents would let her still see Shaney. In an epic victory for Beth, her dad agreed and she'd moved back. This sent me into a bit of a panic. Why hadn't Beth told me this herself? Things were worse than I thought.

Phonecall over, Mum hauled me into a hug that nearly crushed my ribcage. 'Daisy, thank you thank you thank you for not being a nightmare teenager.'

'Gerrroooffff!' I mumbled into her shoulder.

'I mean it,' she said. 'All the stuff you do with River and helping us out with Something Borrowed, you're a star. You haven't given us a minute's trouble since the day you were born. I feel very lucky.'

'I feel lucky too,' my flattened lungs gasped.

It was true. She and Dad pretty much wrote the Laid-back Parenting Bible with their non-judgemental mission statement of Let's Share Everything. My parents, New Age. Beth's parents, Stone Age. No-brainer.

But possessing cool parents was not without its drawbacks, as Mum went on to demonstrate.

'Mainly thank you for not being anything like me when I was sixteen. Bloody hell, when I think back to the mischief me and your dad got up to.'

Her eyes were going worryingly dreamy. 'I

remember this one time, we were thinning the lettuces at Grandad's allotment when the heavens opened. So we nipped in the potting shed to dry off. Well, one thing led to another . . .'

She paused, lost in memory, and that was my cue to fabricate an urgent assignment and run up to my room where I didn't do any homework, but I *did* check my college email.

All hail the Oracle of Ayesha. It was uncanny how often she got things dead right. If it had been the Dark Ages, superstitious peasants would have burned her at the stake. I did indeed have an email from Toby asking me if I fancied 'doing something together' this weekend.

Now, I realised that barring the newly born, ancient and lady-favouring, there wasn't a woman on earth who wouldn't be chewing her own arm off for the chance to go on a date with the God of Gorge that was Toby Smith.

Except me apparently. Obviously, I was some kind of freak. My eyes told me I fancied his frankly spectacular ass off, but my brain had a mind of its own and that was pressing the *thanks, but no thanks button*. Why? Guilt. Ridiculous, pointless *guilt*.

Daisy, you are single. Single. SINGLE. I told myself.

So why did this feel like cheating?

My hands kept reaching for the keyboard and pulling away before my fingertips could hit the *yes please, Toby* keys.

With Ayesha on an overnighter at the observatory with Tom, I tried Beth again. (Still nothing.) Perhaps she was too occupied with her one-woman attempt to break the internet to answer the phone. Seriously, wherever I logged on – Facebook, Twitter, Instagram, Tumblr, Snapchat – there they were, #blessed Beth being #soproud with her #bestboyfriendever #Shaney

Hmmm.

#cheesytags

#spew.

I gazed at the latest photo-splosion of Shaney quitting the pub because he'd passed his personal trainer qualification. Bulging muscles and fake tan don't do it for me, but I'd never seen Beth smilier and I felt a stab of guilt for breaking Rule #2 with my unsupportive bitchy comments.

I tried her number again, but there was still no answer so I logged back on to Facebook to DM her.

And that's when everything changed.

CHAPTER 7

An hour later and my eyes had puffed up to tiny slits. Sad and sore. Mum heard me crying and came up with a cup of tea, but I couldn't drink, couldn't talk about it, couldn't believe what I'd seen.

Beth had just posted another selfie of her and Shaney, so I knew she was online. Comments from loads of the St Mary's crowd were popping up, so I wrote, 'Aw, so cute! Please ring me!!' and was adding heart and champagne emojis when a comment with Matt's name appeared.

And I saw Matt had updated his profile picture.

It wasn't the one I'd taken straight after his last GCSE. The one where he's standing in front of the clock tower at St Mary's, with his tie wrapped round his head punching the air. Not any more.

I bit my lip so hard I tasted blood.

In this new one, he was on a beach, with his arm round a girl. A stunning girl with skin the colour of milk chocolate and a body that lived down the gym. A girl so breathtaking even I fancied her.

Breathe.

Dazed, I flicked to his homepage. More and more and more photos of *my* Matt.

My Matt and this girl sharing a fishbowl cocktail.

My Matt and this girl grinning over tapas.

My Matt and this girl topping up their tans.

She was tagged as 'Rosa Marino', but I couldn't find anything else, except she was Spanish and only ever wore bikinis. Oh, and her profile pic was her lying in a stripy hammock *with Matt.*

Matt clearly wasn't having any issues about moving on. *He* wasn't sitting in his bedroom looking miserable. *He* wasn't in front of his computer feeling too guilty to type 'yes' to a date.

The email! With a sudden sick lurch I realised it must've been to tell me he'd met someone else. Hands shaking, I opened the trash folder, but it was gone.

When I said, *If you leave, it's over,* I thought he'd stay. Then when he left, I thought, *He'll be back soon.* For almost three months I'd been waiting for him to turn up on the doorstep and tell me his body might have been in Spain, but his heart had never left me.

Well, the waiting was over now. This girl had stolen my happy-ever-after.

I carried on clicking through photos until I'd sobbed myself into a lake of snot and tears. Then to really make my night, the crap-top froze, leaving his new girlfriend's flat belly and skinny, hot-dog legs to mock me in full-screen HD.

There was no bright side to this, but at least it solved my dilemma. When the page refreshed, I logged into my college email.

Hi Toby,
I'd absolutely love to.
Daisy x

And this time, I didn't even think twice before I signed off with a kiss.

Screw you, Matt. I thought. *And your hammock*.

After that there could be no drift into blissful unconsciousness. As soon as I closed my eyes, Rosa Marino's impossibly perfect abs were pasted on the inside of my lids, along with Matt's *check this babe out* grin. With a newly lumpy mattress and my pillow apparently stuffed with pebbles, I alternated tossing and turning with fretting and bawling until exhaustion finally tumbled me into a random nightmare.

Me and Matt were eating Babybels in a hammock when Rosa Marino appeared, all rippling uber-abs in a sexy bikini. Giving me the evil eye, she tossed a beanbag from one hand to the other before *smack!* she chucked it in my face, chanting, 'Matt loves *me* to infinity and beyond . . . to infinity and beyond . . . to infinity and bey–'

I woke up, sweaty and panting, to find Buzz Lightyear's helmet hammering on my nose and River's cheesy morning breath sandpapering up my nostrils. 'Get UP, Lazy Daisy! Now!'

Head whirling . . . beanbags, Babybels, bikinis . . . What? Half seven! I rolled River and Buzz off with a squawk and a thud.

Matt's got a new girlfriend.

'Knock knock,' said Dad. 'Cup of tea for my beautiful daughter.'

'She's not here,' I said, dragging the duvet out from under River.

'Daisy threw me on the flooooor,' he wailed.

'Naughty Daisy. I am not your friend.'

'Be a good boy and go downstairs to Mummy,' said Dad, then he sat on the edge of the bed as River stamped out of the room. 'Now, Daisy, I need you to test this recipe for Saturday's cake. Tell me if I've overdone the cinnamon.'

'OK,' I said, tunnelling back out of the duvet because a) he said cake and b) he said cake.

'Do you want to talk?' Dad asked, setting the plate on my bedside table.

'It's pathetic,' I sniffed, shoving my snarled-up, snotty hair out of my face. 'I found out Matt's got a new girlfriend and I . . . I . . .' burst into tears again. 'W-w-why do I care? We're not even togeth-th-ther any moooore.'

Reasons my dad was The Best:
1. Not using the words 'sea', 'fish' or 'plenty'.
2. Bringing me cake.

He gave me a hug. 'Oh, Daisy, love, do you want to stay home and help me sort out this cake? I can ring the college and tell them you're not going in today.'

'No thanks.' I sniffed again and sat up straight. 'I'll be all right. Honest.'

Matt's got a new girlfriend.

Cross my heart, I tried to resist, but my self-control had vanished without a trace. As soon as Dad left, I rebooted the laptop, scrutinising the hammock pic in pixel-point detail, searching for a hint of *I miss Daisy*. But nope: Matt's expression was pride mixed with *phwoooar*, every atom of it directed at the amazing Rosa Marino.

Seriously, I'd never realised abs like that existed outside magazines; she must have done sit-ups at the rate I did lemon drizzle. If I had a figure like hers, I'd have worn a bikini all summer too. Hell, I'd have worn a bikini in the *snow*.

To punch myself in the fragile self-esteem some more, I foolishly decided to examine my own 'flabs' in the shower. Big mistake.

OK, so I'd cut back on footie because of Something Borrowed going mad this year. And obviously my role as Dad's Chief Wedding Cake Tester was hardly conducive to stomach flatness. In fact, today it was mainly conducive to standing in the shower wondering exactly when my belly had turned into uncooked pizza dough.

Dry, dress, then next step: slap. I looked in the mirror and the mirror smirked back, cruelly magnifying my baggy, bloodshot eyes and lunar landscape skin. What a mess. Rosa Marino's HD-ready face flashed before my eyes. As did Matt's smug expression.

Matt's got a new girlfriend.

Decided not to have more cake for breakfast after all.

I had to sprint for the college bus, but (miraculously) made it on time and without any more snotty detours to Blubbering Heights. Tinge of red around the eyes, but no other visible signs I'd only slept for a couple of hours. Inside of course I was a bleak wilderness of emotional devastation.

Badger was in the canteen. 'Hey, Daisy,' he said, putting his copy of *Game of Thrones* face down on the table. 'How's things?'

Part of me wanted to fling my head on his SpongeBob-clad chest and wail *Matt loves someone eeeeelse* until my throat turned inside out. Instead I plonked my butt on to the bench next to him, saying, 'Not bad, thanks. Listen, do you really play the trumpet?'

'Yep, and the trombone, French horn, sax . . . sporadic dabble on the cornet.'

'Wow. Really?' I was genuinely impressed.

'Oh, you know,' he said, going pink, 'not

professionally, but I can knock out a tune.'

'That's totally what I wanted to hear,' I said. 'I know a band that would be very interested in you.' And I relayed Marv 'n' Harv's request for a 'jam'.

'So if I give you Harv's number, you can sort it out, OK?'

'Aye aye, Cap'n,' he said, handing me a mobile so ancient the keypad was in Roman numerals. As I was clunking in the final digit, Toby appeared at our table and there was extreme belly-sucking-in action. (Me, not him.)

'Daisy, hi,' he said as my eyes informed me that that was one tight T-shirt he was covering his muscly fitness with. *Veeery* tight indeed. And *veeery* fit. Oh yes, my heart might've been smashed to pulp, but there was nothing wrong with my eyesight.

'Hi,' I replied. 'How are you?'

'OK. I'll text you about Sunday, shall I?' SpongeBadger interrupted, pocketing his phone and standing up.

'Great,' I said. 'They'll be so pleased.'

'See you later,' he said and drifted off to his next lesson/pineapple under the sea.

'Sunday . . .?' prompted Toby.

I moved my bag on to the floor to create some

sitting-down space. 'He's auditioning for the band my mum sings in. You know Something Borrowed, their wedding business? Something Blue is the band with my Uncle Harvey and his husband, Marvin. Well, I say uncle. Technically he's my godfa–'

'Yes, you told me,' he cut in, still standing and staring after Badger as he disappeared through the exit.

Cringe flashback. *Shut up, Daisy, you bean-spilling fool.*

'Look, I can't stop, I've got physics in a minute,' Toby continued, breaking into a smile. 'Can we decide what we're doing now?'

Matt the Rat and his fab-abbed señorita romped in the Mediterranean sunshine of my memory. A picture postcard with 'He's moved on, now you do the same!' scrawled across it in bold caps.

'Sure,' I said. 'What do you fancy doing?'

'If I pick you up at seven,' he said, 'we can go for something to eat maybe?'

Hmmm. Footie training would mean only an hour left to do hair, make-up and eight million sit-ups, have emergency liposuction and a gastric band fitted.

'Can we make it seven thirty?'

'We can leave it for another day if you want,' he said, holding up his hands in a *whatever* gesture.

'NO! No, it's good. Just I've got training, but it'll be fine. I'll text you my address later.'

'Training?' He tilted his head and looked at me, eyes wide. '*Riiiight*. Seven thirty then. Wear something nice.'

'All my clothes are nice,' I said, smoothing down today's flamingo-print skirt.

Don't know why he laughed (I wasn't being funny), but as he walked off I'm not sure what made me more giddy: the date butterflies or the relief at letting my belly flop back out.

Cripes. A date. Me and Matt used to go to all sorts of places together, but we never called them 'dates' after the first one. Not sure when the official just dating/proper couple crossover point happened. Should I have got a certificate? With Matt it just felt as if we'd always been together.

The first time we went out it was bowling down at The Lord of the Pins. Mum dropped me off; Matt got the bus. I won (four strikes); we sat on the wall outside and shared a bag of crisps and a kiss (both Quaver-flavoured). Not exactly Cupid's finest hour, but good enough to set MattandDaisy in motion for three very, very happy years. At least, that's what *I* thought, although Matt obviously felt differently.

Boyfriends/phones. Same principle. You could constantly search for a better deal (the Beth method) or stay loyal. And I guess I couldn't switch that loyalty off: even though Matt traded me in for a superior model and we were through with a capital HAMMOCK . . . the thought of going out with another guy still freaked me out.

Tonight with Toby would be my second-ever first date. And I needed to get a grip.

I rang Ayesha and she said I just had cold feet. She told me I needed to remember 'men are like horses'.

'Hairy and full of crap?' I said.

Apparently not. She reckoned if you fell off, you needed to ride a new one right away or risk developing terminal crazy-cat-lady syndrome.

I told her that in many, many cases, I actually preferred cats to men. They tended to be cleaner, more affectionate and, on the whole, more interesting company. Furthermore, I disliked the stereotype of the crazy cat lady and its outdated and frankly offensive implication that a woman without a man was in some way sad and unfulfilled.

'What happened to the Number 1 Rule for Girls?' I concluded. 'You know, *It's always better to be single?*'

'Always better to be single *than to date a twat*,' she finished off. 'Is Toby a twat?'

'I don't think so.'

'Well then. If I thought you were going to dive in heart-first like Beth, I'd say don't do it, but it's been three months. You've listened to enough Coldplay.' She patted my arm. 'Remember the F-word? You deserve some shiny, datey FUN. Do you want me to come and do your make-up?'

Horses, cats, whatever cryptic animal analogy Ayesha used, I couldn't argue. I was incredibly nervous and a tiny voice kept (irrationally) whispering, *This is disloyal*. But what was the alternative? Spend every night sobbing into the keyboard while I Googlestalked Matt?

No.

Brace yourself, Toby Smith, I thought. *You and me are off for a 'ride'.*

CHAPTER 8

So it all started quite well. Picturing Matt and his ab-fab lady love inspired me to vamp myself up to the max. Tough to pull off given I'd spent the previous hour chasing a ball across mud with ten feral females, but luckily Ayesha had supercharged her Fairy Glam-mother wand to perform a little dirty-to-flirty miracle.

And a miracle she performed. Even if I say so myself, I scrubbed up pretty pretty.

Crazy hair straightened and up? Check. Individual false eyelashes? Check. Glitter nails? Yeah, baby.

'It's good you decided to go,' Ayesha said, adding the finishing *je ne sais fab* to my make-up. 'Take your mind off You-know-who.'

'How come you never told me about Rosa?' I said. 'You must've known I'd find out.'

'I was going to,' she answered. 'Sssh. Close your eyes.' I felt her brush something across my face. '*Puuurrrrrfect*. I wanted to tell you in person, but you saw those pics before I got chance. Poor you, must've been a surprise.'

'*Ha*. Understatement.'

'You know Matt's gutted you won't answer his emails,' she carried on.

'Answer them? I don't even *read* them. Soon as I see his name, I hit delete.'

'Look up,' she said, wiggling the mascara brush down to the roots. 'Well, maybe you should. It's a shame you can't stay friends at least.'

'You lot can stay friends with him, that's fine. But I don't want to know.'

'The only thing he ever talks to me about is you,' she went on. 'And he says this Rosa girl isn't anything serious.'

I snorted. 'Oh right, so she tripped and fell into that hammock with him, did she?'

Ayesha was blotting my face with powder now. 'Nearly done. I'm just saying, look at it from Matt's perspective. You dump him —'

'He dumped me!'

'Did he or did he not want to keep it going?'

'Yes, but I said if he left we'd be over.'

With an exasperated note creeping into her voice, she said, 'What else could he do? His mum needed help in the bar.'

'I said long-distance relationships never work and, guess what, I was right.'

She tutted and snapped the compact shut. 'You unfriend him, block his mobile number, ignore his emails, refuse to talk to him. What do you expect him to do?'

I reached my hand out for the compact. 'He left. Screw him.' Powder, lipgloss, eyeliner, mints, purse, keys . . . I gathered up the handbag essentials. 'I am not having this conversation. Over and out.'

Ayesha sighed and shook her head. 'Fine. So, Toby Le Handsome then. What's his surname?'

'Smith.'

She went over to my desk, tapped on the keyboard.

'I've already tried that,' I said, spritzing perfume on my wrists.

'Wow,' she said. 'How many hits? Where's he from again?'

'London-ish.'

'There are about a billion profiles for that name.'

Ayesha frowned, peering at the screen. 'Have you got any more details to narrow it down?'

I was wriggling into my dress: a Mum-special, red, satiny, fifties style with a (too?) revealing sweetheart neckline and (too?) figure-hugging, Marilyn Monroe-esque wiggle skirt. With Belly Constrictor control pants working their magic underneath, I was hopeful the overall effect would be seductively clingy rather than just 'too small'.

'Not really. If you're that mad to see what he's like, you can have a look out of the window when he picks me up.' I gave my bra straps a hoick and scrutinised my worryingly wenchified chest. 'Be honest. Does this dress make me look fat?'

'*Fat?*' Scandalised voice. She closed the lid of my laptop and turned round. 'Don't be ridiculous. Nothing could make you look fat.'

'What about my bum?' I said, twisting round in front of the mirror. 'And my belly.'

'Listen carefully,' she said, folding her arms and speaking *veeery* slowly. 'Your bum is not fat. Neither is your belly. Or your elbows, knees, your ears or any other part of your anatomy. Get it? The only part of you that's fat is your imagination.'

She came over and stood by me at the mirror. 'Girlfriend, you put the YOU in Be-YOU-tiful. Just be your wonderful true self tonight and Toby Wotsit will feel like a man with six balls.'

Blink.

'On the Lotto.'

Ah.

She parked herself on my bed. 'Any idea where you're going?'

'No, he just said 'nice' and 'food', so I'm thinking not doner and chips at Abra-kebab-ra.' This was Matt's favourite eatery, not mine, and I had my fingers crossed it wouldn't be Toby's either. But even that stray thought gave me a tiny treacherous pang.

'Come on then, spill the deets,' she continued as I held different earrings up. 'What do you actually know about him?'

'Er, he lives with his mum?'

'OK.'

'And her boyfriend.'

'Go on.'

'Nice car.'

'And . . .?'

'Um, he's really fit?'

'And . . .?'

'That's as far as I've got really.'

'Seriously?'

'What, I should've asked for his CV?' I held the earrings in front of her. 'Now tell me: hoops or hearts?'

Then, at the sound of a car pulling up outside, I leaned over to lift the blind a fraction (yep, black mini) and squealed, 'It's him! He's here!'

Ayesha giggled and joined me, two pairs of sneaky eyeballs peeking through the slats as Toby got out and leaned against the car, holding his phone.

'OM genuine G,' said Ayesha in a hushed tone. 'Where'd you find him? The perfect aisle at Boys R Us?'

Have to admit, at that, my much-squashed ego shook its feathers out for a strut.

'Obviously don't tell anyone I said that,' she added quickly, gazing down. 'Actually, maybe you could bring him to Tom's eighteenth.'

'You think he's all right then?'

'I . . . erm . . . what?'

'Ayesha, are you dribbling?'

She wiped her sleeve absently-mindedly over the windowsill as my phone beeped: **Outside Tx** and my insides lurched in a way they hadn't since Mum last cooked mung beans.

'Hearts,' said Ayesha, pointing at my ears, and I hooked them in as we went downstairs.

'Back by ten, please,' said Mum, straightening the collar on my jacket. 'Early start for the wedding tomorrow, remember.'

'Have a lovely time,' said Dad.

'Call me,' said Ayesha with a cheesy thumbs up and grin combo.

'I can see your booooobies!' said River.

Heaving the front of the dress up (again), I took a deep breath and stepped outside.

'Well, don't you look glamorous.' Toby held my elbow as he leaned in to give me a kiss on the cheek that sent my jelly-belly intestines as aflutter as the Belly Constrictors allowed. He opened the car door.

'Thanks,' I said, trying to gracefully slide in to the passenger seat.

Behind the wheel now, he was gazing at me in *exactly* the same way Matt used to gaze at his Friday night Abra-kebab-ra: lingeringly, lovingly and with a not-very-disguised desire to get stuck in.

'Unusual dress,' he said with a smirk. 'Really shows off your . . . *eyes*.'

Cheeky. He'd started the engine now and we were leaving my street behind, turning off on to the main road.

'Thanks, my mum made it. You look nice too.' Official Understatement of the Century: the guy rocked a tight tee like no mere mortal should. 'So, where are we going?'

'Blanco. I've booked us a table.'

I only just managed to stop my jaw hitting the floor with a cartoony thud.

'Have you been before?' he continued.

Hang-out of the nipped, ripped and surgically lipped soap star/footballer/wannabe glamour model crowd? *That* Blanco. Ha. Matt thought Nando's was splashing out.

'Not exactly. Heard of it though,' I said.

'You'll love it, trust me.'

And I did.

We were led to a white, velvet-lined private booth by 'Fernando', a waiter so handsome he made my eyeballs gasp. The rest of the staff weren't too shabby either, eight foot tall with digitally enhanced skin, teeth and hair. If any scientists were planning an upgrade of the human race in the near future, free templates were available here.

'*Buenas tardes, señorita*. Dreenk?' the superhuman drawled.

'Diet Coke, please.'

'Ugh! We do not 'ave *Diet Coke* at Blanco,' he said, facially emoting *filtheee peasant*. 'Blanco is purit-aaay. Blanco is white-aaay.'

White-aaay?!

'Er, OK, can I have . . .'

What? Lightly chilled unicorn tears? Freshly squeezed swan soul? The Elixir of Life filtered through an angel's wing?

'Two elderflower pressés, please,' finished Toby and I smiled gratefully as the waiter glided off.

He gazed round the room. 'So, what do you think of this place?'

'It's beautiful,' I said.

'It is, isn't it? So clean and simple. You know, they only serve white food and drink.'

'I got that. Why?'

'So nothing interrupts the designer's vision. Apparently.'

The place was cool enough to make my teeth ache in fact. Chandeliers, abstract art, square plates and white EVERYTHING. Striking . . . but too try-hard for my taste. I was more a cheery clutter and colour chick. Truthfully, I reckoned the decorator's brief may have been 'pretentious operating theatre with a hint of morgue'.

The food options continued this blob of nonsense: moon-harvested mushrooms in Sauvignon sauce, Peruvian white truffles, whipped white chocolate ganache with an elderflower spray. Pan-fried Arctic fox on a bed of fluffed-up summer clouds with a snowflake foam . . . (possibly).

With any of my friends, I'd've been unleashing a load of gibberish guffaw by now, but Toby seemed to have bought into the 'Blanco Vision' as described on the cover of 'The Concept Guide' (or as I usually called it, 'The Menu').

'The clarity of virginal cuisine against the backdrop of bleached bone china allows explicit focus on the mélange of flavours, without distraction. A sensation explosion for the palate but for the eyes, a soothing meditation.'

'*Virginal* cuisine?'

I tried not to snigger as Toby read out this culinary

Emperor's New Clothes-esque drivel. Then he grinned. 'Do you think anyone genuinely falls for that?'

'*Ye-e-es*,' I said, with an inner phew he wasn't one of them. 'People too dim to realise white velvet seats are a pain to keep clean. White food, clean chairs.'

'Ah, so what it should really say is "a pretentious hook for the gullible, but for the cleaners, an easy job"?'

I laughed. 'That is exactly right. Actually, did you write this? Is that how you got us in at short notice?'

Mood-flip. Ignoring my questions, he reached across the table, taking hold of my hand. 'I chose it for you because it's pure and simple, like daisies. And totally unique.'

Crikey.

'You know, you're so beautiful, I can't stop staring at you.' He leaned in towards me. 'And I've been dying to do this all night.'

I froze, but he wasn't going in for the kiss. Instead, he reached up behind my head and, pulling out the clips, fluffed out my blonde hair.

'Your hair is just incredible,' he said. 'It was the first thing I noticed when you walked into tutorial. You shouldn't hide it away.'

I was thinking, *Bloody hell, that took ages to put up!*

but then I saw he had the same *I can't believe my luck* expression as Matt in the hammock pic. I was half expecting to wake up to find Buzz Lightyear whacking me round the face.

But the pinch-me-I'm-dreaming sensation didn't fade as the evening went on. Toby ordered for both of us, on the basis he 'knew his way round the menu' and when our snooty waiter performed the Ceremony of Presentation (served the food), I realised he was right: each course was more delish than the last.

Unfortunately, by this point the waistband of my Belly Constrictors had rolled down, turning them into a kind of DIY gastric band. An excellent lifehack for anyone who's after a cheap alternative to weight-loss surgery. Less excellent when it came to actually eating.

And when Fernando performed the Ceremony of Illumination (lit the candles) and the bouncing light glittered in reflected sparkles off the booth's walls, the morgue-y aspect transformed into an enchanted crystal cave. Magical.

But beating the decor, topping the demigod staff, even above the supreme wowness of actually eating in a place like Blanco, was being here with Toby.

Bubbles of *this could be the start of something big* fizzed through me as he listened while I burbled on, and I don't mean in the way most boys seemed to (75 per cent of their mind on Town's chances in the cup and 25 per cent on your boobs). *Actively* listened, leaning forward, eyes on mine as if he thought I was the most fascinating creature on earth, even when I was talking absolute drivel.

'So, let me get this right, you're doing English lit., Spanish and sociology?'

'And tutorial. And maths resit.' I screwed my face up: that word tasted *nasty*.

'You didn't pass maths GCSE?' he said with a *you're not toilet trained* level of shock.

'Don't. I feel such a dumbass. Got five As and four Bs and then a D in maths.'

'Bad paper? Not enough revision?'

I snorted. 'You're joking. I could've been revising maths in the *womb* and I'd still have failed. My head doesn't do numbers. Plus me and my maths teacher never hit it off.'

'I can help you, if you want,' he said, draining the last of his white tea. 'Tutor you.'

'Thanks for the offer, but you'd be wasting your time. I've been told I'm a lost cause.'

'Can you keep a secret?' His voice dropped to a whisper that forced me to lean close in. It felt like how I imagined downing a glass of champagne while simultaneously falling down a lift shaft would. *Giddy swoopy swoosh.*

'My secret is . . .'

With only centimetres of space between us, I had to grip the arms of the chair to stop the vertigo, the whole thought-translates-to-speech thing beyond me.

'That I am . . .' He did a comedy look-about, eyes side to side, as if to check no one would overhear. 'A maths geek.'

I faked a shock-horror tone. 'No way!'

'Seriously. Nerd is the word. GCSE grade A in Year 9. Full marks at A level in Year 11. So you see,' I could feel his breath on my ear, 'I will tutor you and I promise you will pass your maths. And, one thing you should know about me, Daisy, is I never, *ever* break a promise.'

Perhaps, in the next phase of evolution, oiled castors would replace feet. In which case, our waiter was well ahead of the game. The git.

He skated silently up. 'More to dreenk?' And like that, he smashed our intimo moment with a knowing smirk.

Toby checked his watch. 'Daisy, it's half nine now. We need to make a move. Can I have the bill, please?'

I unhooked my bag off the chair, Toby blatantly *heh-heh-ing* as I pulled out my Hello Kitty purse.

'I'm getting this,' he said before I'd even opened it.

'No, that's not fair. We can go halves.'

'Seriously, Daisy, my shout,' he insisted, sticking little Kitty straight in his pocket.

'Hey!' I reached towards him, but then what? Would I grapple with his trouser region?

Actually . . .

'You can have it back when we're in the car,' he said. 'No arguments.'

'Well, I'm paying next time,' I said feebly.

I popped to 'powder my nose' (aka wrestle with the Pants of Pain) while he paid the bill. Then we left the restaurant, me floating down the street on a frothy cloud of happiness past 'Fernando' who was taking a break outside. Puffing on the *purit-aaay* of a stinking roll-up as he chatted on the phone, his accent now about as authentically Spanish as a Yorkshire pudding. The dirty hypocrite.

Still, this was definitely shaping up as a nominee for second Best-First-Date Ever and twinkly thoughts of the future were being born on the journey home. And as we parked up outside my house, I was happier than I'd been since Matt left.

'Here I am: Home Sweet Home!' I chirped in the manner of a fifties housewife. Or a complete simpleton. 'Thanks for the lift. And dinner. What a great place, I loved it.'

This was it.

Eeek.

For the first time in three years, I was experiencing the *to snog or not to snog?* date scenario that had last involved a bag of cheesy snacks and the former love of my life.

'I've had a great night, Daisy,' Toby said, shifting in his seat to face me.

'Me too,' I said, heart trying to burst through my ribcage.

'I'd love to do it again.'

He was looking at me intently, intensely. For the first time in weeks, months, *years* even, Matt wasn't at the front of my mind. I briefly pictured his face, then pushed it away. Time to stop punishing myself by raking over the past, wishing I'd behaved differently. I wasn't reliving old memories now; I was making new ones and Toby could be the new man for the new me. Matt had Rosa, why couldn't I have Toby?

'God, you're so beautiful,' he whispered, and his words shot thrills through me. 'I can't wait to see you again and you haven't even gone yet.'

I held my breath and my eyes started closing for the inevitable; my pulse was pounding, my body acting on instinct as my head tilted. With our lips almost touching, my last conscious thought was, *Maybe I shouldn't have had those garlic mushrooms . . .*

'See you tomorrow?' he whispered.

Yesss! . . . Noooooo! The wedding. 'Sorry, I'm busy. Working, remember?'

'Can't you get out of it?'

'Sorry, I promised.'

This was followed by a nanosecond's pause before my lips were making sweet solo lurve to the air. Pop went the bliss bubble and I fell to earth with a thump while Toby sat back in his seat. 'No problem.'

Could I give work a miss? I had a brief conscience tussle, but no; I couldn't leave Mum and Dad in the lurch.

'You know I'd love to,' I said, 'but I've promised my parents and they'll be knackered if I don't help out.'

'Sure,' he said.

'Yeah, this one's the full package: dress, decor, photos, band. Big schmooze for more bookings.'

'Where is it again?'

'Glenside Hall, couple of miles out of town. Sorry, it's a really big deal or I'd ask for the day off.'

'Well, I hope everything goes well,' he said, 'subtly' jingling the keys in the ignition. 'Maybe some other time.'

The electric atmosphere had fizzled to nothing and with Mr Chivalry clearly having left the building right behind Ms Sorry-I'm-Busy, I opened the door myself.

'Thanks again for a nice night,' he said through the open window. 'And Daisy?'

'Yes?'

'Don't take this the wrong way – you look amazing. But you're so pretty, you honestly don't need to, you know, do *this* for my benefit.' And he waved his hand at my chest area. Then he drove off leaving me standing on the pavement thinking, *Do what?*

I let myself in and walked straight into Mum who was hovering in the hall. (As in waiting, not levitating.)

'Tell me you haven't been there all night,' I said.

'Course not. I heard the car. How was it? Did you have a good time?'

But I'd paused to look at myself in the hall mirror. *Norks ahoy!* my reflection wolf-whistled.

Hmmmm. I'd had that tiny *Is this OTT?* wobble when I first put the dress on, but still . . . had Toby really just boob-shamed me? How mortifying.

'Mum, be honest. Do you think this dress is tarty?'

She looked surprised. 'No, it's lovely. You look gorgeous.'

'Thanks, I do, don't I?' I agreed.

Yes, Toby Smith. If the view south of my neck offends you, feel free to look elsewhere. And I dress for my benefit, not yours.

'So come on, tell me. Where'd you go?' Mum asked eagerly.

'Blanco.'

'Oooh, posh,' she said. 'And how was Toby?'

'Oh, you know. Nice,' I said. *And gorgeous. Funny. Interesting. Clever.*

Intense.

She followed me into the kitchen. 'And the food?'

'Small,' I answered, homing in on the fridge.

'But you had a good time?'

'Yeah, I guess. Tired now.'

'Well, I'm glad you had fun,' she said with a hug and an ease off the Inquisition. 'I'm off to bed. Dad made you a pie, if you're hungry. Don't wake River when you come up and remember we're out early tomorrow, please.'

In the fridge was an apple pie with my name on it. (Literally, in pastry letters.)

Mmmmmm.

And a pot of cream.

Best. Dad. Ever.

I was that hungry post-Blanco I could have eaten the *fridge*, never mind its contents. We held no truck with sparrow portions in the Green household, so I tugged, shucked and finally hopped the Belly Constrictors down to my knees to create the necessary space.

The relief! Almost worth wearing them just for the bliss of taking them off.

And I could always burn the pie off playing extra footie. Maybe I could have a game of Frisbee with River. Plus, working the wedding would burn enough calories for ten apple pies and –

Oh, who was I kidding? All I was really thinking about was Toby. And the text I'd sent while I heated up the pie. The one he hadn't replied to.

Thanks for a lovely night. I'll pay next time! Daisy x

I wasn't snarky or feisty, so I don't get why he hadn't answered.

Maybe it was just a one-date stand after all.

CHAPTER 9

I was woken up early by my phone ringing.

Matt!

No.

Toby!

My right leg shot to attention. My left leg, however, chose to stay in bed, causing me to face-plant the carpet. Ouch. Still tangled in the duvet, I managed a commando crawl across the floor to the jingling Holy Grail. Reached up, plucked it off the desk and . . .

Ayesha.

'Oh, it's you.'

'Love you too, babes,' she said.

'Sorry.' I untangled myself and sat back on the bed. 'I'm aching all over,' I sighed, checking my nose for chafage. *Ow. Tender.*

'Heavy night?'

'Humph. Not so much as a snog. Had to be home by ten.'

I put her on speaker and had a quick scroll on the vague chance I'd slept through a text alert, but there was nothing. So this is what happens when you raise your portcullis to a knight in shining armour: the invading forces swarm and trample all over your emotional ramparts.

'So . . .?' she prompted.

'So what?' I said.

'I've only got a minute, I'm supposed to be helping Mum. What do you think, woman? Spill your beans!'

'Dinner at Blanco.'

'Seriously?' Squeal! 'Wow, he must be keen. I wanted to go for Tom's eighteenth, but his mum said it cost too much. How was it? Did you see any celebs?'

I filled her in on the decor, the food and the scary waiters. Did toy with the idea of sharing Toby's feedback on my neckline, but I didn't want to press Ayesha's feminist buttons and anyway it was kind of a backwards compliment really because he was saying I was naturally pretty. I guess.

Apart from that teeny omission, she got the unedited

very-hot-to-suddenly-not date experience.

'What do you mean "distant"?' she said.

'Distant, as in not close. Apart. One minute he's leaning in, set to lock lips. Next thing, he's leaping away.'

'Daisy, be honest,' she said, 'did your breath stink?'

'NO!' Although, hmmmm, garlic mushrooms . . .

'Does sounds fairly schizoid then,' she said.

'Seriously, it was a dream date right till I told him I'd got to work today. That's when he went all Ice Ice Baby on me.'

'Oh well, at least you got a free dinner,' she said, practical as ever. 'And who else do we know who's been to Blanco? I am well jealous.'

'Yeah, suppose,' I sighed.

'You could always think of Toby as a dry run. Greasing your saddle, as it were, before you find the right horse.'

'But that's it,' I said, passionately flinging myself back on the bed. 'I know I was flip-floppering about going in the first place, but . . . something changed, I don't know what. Like I think he could be the right horse.

'We had this real connection in the restaurant, I could feel it. Then when we almost kissed in the car, *whoa*. I can't describe the chemistry, it was incredible. Almost *nuclear*. It was as if —'

103

'Daisy, we need to get going soon,' Mum shouted up the stairs.

'It was as if . . .' I repeated, half to myself, hugging my Hello Kitty pyjama case.

'Daisyyyyy.'

'Ring me later,' Ayesha said. 'Hope the wedding's a success. And try not to worry: if it's meant to happen then it will.'

And I'd been trying ever since to finish my sentence. It was as if . . . what? We were in a bubble of light? A megawatt spotlight was illuminating the two of us? Until Toby pulled the plug. Fireworks to fizzlement.

How could two people share an identical experience, but take completely different things from it? Same time, same place, same big chemistry zinging between us like a . . . big chemistry zinging thing, but apparently only one set of twinkly future thoughts.

We dropped River off at Nana Green's then set off for the hall. Driving along, Mum and Dad were verbally ticking off the to-do list and I was *uh-huhing* in the right places, but my mind was too stuffed with boy business to pay proper attention. In actual fact I'd clocked off somewhere between 'spare bunting' and 'emergency mop bucket'.

As we turned up the long driveway I braced myself for a day of a) hectic work and b) acutely missing Matt in his capacity as work colleague. Separating lairy guests, unblocking a Portaloo, coaxing a sulky pageboy – whatever random disaster the occasion threw at him, Matt always had it nailed. Mum and Dad really needed to replace him before the three of us died of exhaustion.

And, yep, this one was shaping up to be a dashing around go go go from the get-go. What with fixing wonky table decorations and topping up droopy blooms, by the time Zayn (aka Dream Groom) was standing under the peony arch eagerly waiting his soon-to-be wife's entrance, dwelling on Toby had taken a back seat.

Something Borrowed was our livelihood, but Mum poured her heart into it and it was her cute details that made us stand out. Like suggesting *both* parents walk the bride up the aisle.

'She's giving herself away,' Mum would say, 'but the two of you brought her up so maybe the two of you should be with her now.' And today, along with the sweet flower-girl leading with the bouquet, that had the guests reaching for their hankies before the first words were out.

Listening to the couple's vows had *me* filling up

and I didn't even know them. They were so simple and heartfelt, about how they'd met at school and known they'd always be inseparable. Just like Mum and Dad. Blub.

Altar-wise, I'd seen the lot: shakes, tears, faints, gurgles, giggles and (once, memorably) a vomiting vicar. But Zayn and Alice? Not a trace of nerves. Not a hint of waver. They simply stood there gazing at each other, as if they'd spent their whole lives on a path to this moment. And as they kissed I clapped so hard my palms were stinging.

I promise to walk wherever you go.

I promise to hold your hand in the sunshine and the rain.

This was the future I'd planned with Matt, the path paved with love that would lead from Year 9 Quaversnog to a flower-strewn altar. This was the future he'd destroyed, of course, when he picked *Magaluf* over me.

Maga-sodding-luf. Where the streets were paved with spew.

Between Matt's murder of my romantic vision and Toby's continuing a-textuality, I could very easily have slid into deep misery. But this was Alice and Zayn's wedding and that meant I was very, *very* busy. I pasted my professional smile on and hit it flat out, buzzing around like a blue-assed fly, determined to make the day unforgettable for all the right reasons. And before I knew it, the evening reception was beginning.

Rule #6 commanded: *Dress to make yourself happy* and in this frock of fabulousness, I was definitely following orders. Drop-waisted dresses were usually a no-no for me on account of my bosoms, but thanks to Mum's needle-magic, this silver number fitted perfectly. That bugle bead detailing had taken hours, but one spangly swish under the dancing lights and every finger-pricking second was worth it.

Only had time for a quick swipe of mascara and lipgloss, but with Mum's silk shawl over my shoulders and my hair swept up in a clip, lack of slap didn't matter. Not that anyone was even glancing my way of course. Not with Alice and Zayn's Look of Love outdazzling the spotlights.

I was moving from table to table now, helping the waiting staff to clear away the many champagne bottle empties (and, I admit it, checking my phone for Toby news for approx. the 326th time) when I heard Marv's voice over the microphone.

'Ladieeees and gentlemeeeen, please be upstanding for the first dance.'

Harv started frantically waving at Mum, who was adjusting Alice's antique lace veil. I put my phone in my bag and rushed to take her place.

Oh, that dress. One of Mum's best ever: an ivory satin, flare-sleeved twenties design embroidered with beaded wildflowers, every gorgeous stitch a tiny work of art.

Mum's biggest talent (I thought) was her vision. She saw the hidden beauty in a tired old dress no one wanted. She designed, she ripped, she cut, she sewed and put it together in exactly the perfect way. A picture could make a room look nice, but my mum created art that decorated people.

Artists had it easier really, what with canvases being pretty much identically flat and rectangular and people generally not. My genius mum made every bride beautiful, no matter what her shape.

I made sure Alice's veil was impeccable as Mum stepped up onstage, seconds before the bride and groom swept on to the dance floor. And the finishing touch? Tiny shiny butterflies and dragonflies fluttering in silvery shadows around the walls as Mum flicked the switch on the projector.

The room held its breath as Marv counted them in on the drums. Mum held the microphone stand and started to sing.

'*I don't know what it is that makes me love you so.*'

Stage lights muted, the spotlight followed the bride and groom dancing in perfect rhythm to Mum's smoky voice. Even over the band I could hear a wave of ooohs and aaaahs from the guests.

I'd shifted into work autopilot now. Disco, photo booth, box up the cake slices, clear up, home: I knew exactly how the evening would pan out now.

Or at least I thought I did.

Until six foot two of Scarily Handsome Surprise walked in.

I squinted through the semi-darkness to where this new guest now had both elbows resting on the bar. Film-star face topped with a mop of black floppy hair. Silver butterflies flitting across a bright white T-shirt. My heart did a backflip.

Toby? Here?

Every gaze was trained on the bride and groom, suspended in a moment of perfect happiness as they danced to the band. Every gaze, that is, except mine . . . and Toby's.

Dad was snapping away and I carried on tailing him, but each time my eyes flicked to the bar, there he was, Mr Tall Dark and Cocky. Leaning back, with a hint of a grin across his symmetrical features. Literally no one was as symmetrical as Toby. It was unnatural: those cheekbones must have been mapped out with a set square.

Then the bride and groom were sweeping into a flourish and as the woohooing built to a crescendo, the band took a bow. Dad clapped, beaming with love and pride as Mum blew him a kiss. No doubt about it, love was in the air tonight and my lungs were currently inhaling a mix of one part oxygen to two parts romance.

'Can I go off for five minutes?' I whispered. 'Have a break?'

'Course,' Dad said, polishing the camera lens. 'But not too long, Daze. I can start the photo booth off, but I'll need to go when they cut the cake.'

Dodging drunken uncles and hammered grannies, I slalomed my way through the crowd to where Toby was adorning the bar, rocking back on his heels and looking so incredibly, scarily handsome that I don't care what the laws of biology say, my heart was tumbling for Team GB while I prayed: *Dear God, if you stop me visibly sweating in this dress, I swear I will never, ever be mean about any of Beth's boyfriends again. Amen.*

'Hi,' Toby said, kissing me on the cheek. 'Thought I'd come by and say sorry I didn't call. I've had a crazy day.'

'It's fine,' I lied. 'Me too. Been busy, I mean.'

'So this is what your mum and dad do for a living,' he said. 'Organise other people's weddings.'

'Yes.'

'What do you do?'

'Oh, everything really. Mainly that.' I gestured over to where Dad was at the booth. 'The guests get the fancy-dress stuff and props out and I take the pictures. It's just a bit of fun, but it's dead popular.'

'Nice. And that's your dad over there?'

'Yes.'

'That's your mum up with the band?'

'Yep. Just till the DJ takes over.'

'Cool, I can see where you get your hair from,' he said, leaning in to tug a strand free. 'Did you inherit her voice too?'

I laughed. 'God, no. My Nana Green says I sing like a cat with its plums caught in a mangle.'

Plums? Aaaargh! Dorothy Parker and Oscar Wilde slowly rotated in their graves. Toby cracked a *riiiight* smile and I cringed, yet again wondering what it was about him that caused this brain-to-mouth breakdown.

Then he was gazing intently at me again, like in Blanco. Really intently. Perhaps *too* intently, in a way that caused (please God, no!) bogey panic. I sniffed and dipped my head slightly, as a precaution.

He lifted my chin, while entirely misunderstanding. 'You're not mad at me for turning up, are you?' His gaze flicked over me, from my silver ballet flats to my pinned-up hair. 'You look absolutely stunning tonight. About a thousand times prettier without all that make-up on.'

Technically I was wearing *some*, but if he wanted to think I was *au naturel* and 'stunning', that was fine by me.

When we were together, Matt lobbed me a very occasional, 'You look nice, babes.' I wondered if he ever dazzled Rosa Marino with physique-based compliments. I bet he sat in his mum's bar when it was quiet, writing odes to her abs and sonnets to her —

Forget. About. Matt.

'Er, cheers,' I said to Toby. (Responding to appearance-based compliments being an area I needed to work on. Along with forgetting about Matt.)

'Shall we slope off somewhere then?' he said.

'Actually, I'd better find my dad,' I said, scanning the room.

'Is it OK if I hang around?' he said. 'That dress is beautiful by the way.'

'Thanks, my mum made it.' I said, mentally adding, *Same as she did the red Maz Monroe number you boob-dissed. And which I still love.*

'What time do you finish?'

We watched as Granny and Grandpa Groove nimbled past us en route to where the DJ had begun blasting out disco classics.

'I've a feeling it's going to be a late one,' I said.

I made my way back to the photo booth where Dad had been replaced by Mum, who was in her element persuading an elderly lady she would totally rock a Madonna conical bra. And because she was made of awesomeness, she didn't hiss, *Where have you been?* Or give me daggers.

Instead she went, 'It's OK, love. We're done now the DJ's here, so Marv and Harv have been giving me a hand. We're having a ball, aren't we, Irene?'

Irene/Madonna thrust her fluorescent truncheon at Harv with a leer. He inched towards Marv.

'Who's that at the bar?' Mum said.

'Toby.'

'Toby dinner-date Toby?'

'That's the one.'

She craned her neck to get another peek. 'Oooh, he's lovely,' she said. 'Well, we can manage here for a while if you want to go and talk to him.'

Bless her. Filled from the curls to the toe topful of happy hippy loveliness.

'Cheers, Mum. I'll be back soon,' I promised and headed over to where Toby's A-list handsomeness was attracting some lustful lady stares.

'That was quick,' he said, in a pleased voice that made my tummy flip.

'Not finished for the night, just got an extended break,' I said, fighting the crazed *I can't believe you're here!* grin that was threatening to take over my face. 'Mum and Marv and Harv are going to sort it between them, so I can –'

'Come for a walk with me. It's too loud to talk properly.' He grabbed my hand and led me through the crowd of smokers 'n' vapers huddled round the emergency exit and out into the night.

Onscreen starry strolls were so romantic and I desperately tried to channel that vibe, I swear. Me and Toby, bathed in moonlight in the grounds of costume-drama town like a twenty-first century Lizzy B and Mr

D. Stashing secret notes in the shrubbery, exchanging lingering glances over the herbaceous borders while indoors, a kitchen maid roasted an urchin or two for our supper . . .

Even though Toby had apparently organised a full moon for the occasion, it was the lanterns lining the path that illuminated our way. It wouldn't have surprised me to hear a string quartet strike up from behind a bush with a heavenly chorus of nightingales singing for us and us alone. Love among the lilies. Idyllic. Perfect. And him turning up out of the blue! Be still my leaping heart.

The stars were fairy lights sprinkled across the sky and flowers perfumed the air of this romantic DisneyDaisyworld stage.

Meanwhile, here in Realworld, my lips were turning mauve and I was shivering like a dying Brontë. It was only September, but a chilly snap in the air plus this flimsy dress made it feel like we'd stepped through that fire exit and into Narnia where Queen Icicle Knickers was racing across the snowy plains in a sleigh driven by four polar bears, and I feared for my frostbitten foof.

'Silver really suits you,' Toby said over the sound of my teeth chattering. 'I mean, you look good in everything, but I love you in this. That red dress was a bit . . .'

?????

'A bit loud,' he concluded. 'But silver makes you look . . . ethereal. Angelic in the moonlight.'

Okaaaay. Full marks for poetic vocab, but suddenly all I could think of was graveyards and creepy statues. Erm, not what a girl needed in what I now realised was a lonely, dark place with a semi-stranger. I was suddenly very conscious I hardly knew anything about him. And what was that with not even finding him online?

I'd seen a lot of horror movies in my time; I knew the score. My teeth chattered. My knees knocked.

Toby took his jacket off and put it round my shoulders. Heavy, expensive, almost certainly dry clean only. A discreet pat round revealed no hidden rubber gloves/ bin bags/axe, reassuringly suggesting 'dismembering Daisy' probably wasn't on the agenda.

'How come you came here tonight?' I asked.

He turned to face me. 'Why do you think? I wanted to see you. And . . .' He paused. 'To say sorry about going off radar. It was full on when I got home last night and, well, it's complicated.'

'Why? What's happened?'

'Come on, let's sit down,' he said, leading me to a bench in a sheltered alcove.

I pulled his jacket tighter round my shoulders as he continued. 'It's no major drama, you know, my home stuff. Very boring.'

He casually rested his arm along the back of the bench and I got the swirly, swoopy sensation again. Oh God, the smell of him: lemon mixed with spiced fruit. That hint of vanilla and cotton along with the weight of his arm against me and the warmth radiating from his body. Yep, absolutely the last sensation I was feeling was bored.

Then he looked at me. I looked at him. He put both arms round me and I *knew* it was going to happen. The big what-almost-happened in the car last night. Me, him and the moonlight cosmically aligned for a textbook kiss scenario. Infinitely more fun than a) a chat about his domestic problems and b) being chopped into tiny pieces.

He leaned in closer and I leaned in closer until *POW.* It was just me and him in the dark night, kissing, both of us absolutely on the same page now. And it felt so *right.* My entire body tingled with the rightness of it.

Except my outraged conscience, which was hissing, *How dare you kiss someone who isn't Matt?*

I visualised Matt 'moving on' with his new stick lady love. That did the trick.

Shut up, conscience.

Arms that weren't Matt's held me tight; lips that weren't Matt's were pressed against mine: anatomically identical, but emotionally miles apart.

Then Toby's hand was stroking the back of my head and (again) undoing the clip to run his fingers through my hair. And I only had a fleeting second of *Has he got a hair fetish?* Followed by *I really hope his hands don't get stuck* before I was melting into the whole whirly, spinny thrill of the moment.

If Toby could bottle whatever it is he has, he'd be the richest man on earth. That mesmerising aura just intensified the nearer I got and I was pretty darn close now. Spellbinding from a distance, intoxicating close up and this first non-Matt kiss was weird, but it was also exciting and completely, completely hypnotic. Little sparks of happiness were surging through me and MattandDaisy suddenly seemed very far away.

Which was why I never heard footsteps coming up the path or sensed a human presence closing in on our bench. Nope, totally caught in the moment, I had no clue until we were interrupted by a stagey 'ahem'. I leapt off Toby like I'd been electrocuted.

Oh, earth swallow me whole: it was Harv.

'Er, Daisy,' he half coughed, making intense eye contact with the ground. 'Sorry to, um, interrupt. Your mum's saying please can you come back and help with the, er . . .'

'Yes! Of course. Straightaway,' I said quickly. 'Thanks, Harv.'

If Toby was fazed by the sudden interruption, he didn't show it. 'I need to get going now, anyway,' he said and stood up.

Nooooo! 'I'm sure this won't go on for too much longer,' I said, trying to stall him. But he already had his car keys in his hand.

'It's OK,' he answered, slipping his jacket off my shoulders. 'You go and help your parents and I'll ring you tomorrow, yeah?'

'Yeah, sure,' Feeling suddenly shy, my voice was quiet. 'And thanks for turning up. It was a nice surprise.'

He whispered in my ear, 'It was totally worth it. I'll call you in the morning.' And with a squeeze of my hand, he vanished into the moonlit night.

Before I could cope with the party mayhem I needed a minute to float back down to the real world, leaning against the wall and grinning à la total loony tunes. Then

I quickly pinned my hair up as best I could and went back inside.

Eeek. Ayesha had got things spot on yet again: spending time with Toby *was* the perfect way to take my mind off Matt. Finally, it looked like *Think positive* was starting to pay off.

CHAPTER 10

Next morning, true to his word, Toby called.

'Hey, gorgeous, how are you doing?'

Normally, it was River prising my eyelids open or poking tiny plastic soldiers in my hair that dragged me from sleep, not the honeyed tones of a bona fide Love God. Today, however, was different and those words were an alarm call I could very easily have got used to. My smile almost split my face apart.

'Hey, yourself,' I said, snuggling deeper into bed as I held the phone to my ear. 'You OK?'

'I'm good,' he said, 'but I'd be even better if I could see you in person. You busy?'

'Erm . . . no.'

'Pick you up at ten then.'

That left me with what . . . forty-seven minutes?

Hmmmm. Pushing it, but theoretically possible. 'Sure,' I said with a flutter of excitement.

The wedding party had gone on until past midnight and that, along with the after-hours clean-up, meant I was feeling significantly more Beast than Beauty this morning.

I heaved myself out of bed and braved opening just one eye in front of the mirror. The grey-skinned Corpse Bride winked back. Yep, they didn't call it beauty sleep for nothing.

In the interests of maximising my forty-seven-and-counting minutes, I dumped half a bottle of conditioner on my parched hair and shaved my legs simultaneously. (And by shaved I mean shredded. Mental note: certain tasks should not be multied.) Then I virtually scrubbed my epidermis off with zesty, grainy stuff in an attempt to restore a little human vitality.

Added to this was my, *ugh*, serious dead person breath. I brushed my minging gnashers then gargled mouthwash through two complete verses of 'Thriller'. Busted some mean zombie dance moves in front of the bathroom mirror while I was at it and – *shazam!* – at least I wouldn't knock him unconscious when I opened my mouth.

Phase two of the Resurrection involved everything my dressing table had to offer. Only the miracle of make-up could raise me from the dead and I went at it like a surgeon preparing to operate. Primer? Check. Highlighter? Check. Concealer? More concealer? Blusher? Bronzer? Lipgloss? Check check checkity check.

My hair still had a slight crunchiness despite the conditioner. No time for the straighteners, but twisting it into a topknot disguised the last of the frizz. Final stage was wardrobe. Nothing black (too draining), red (too bright), green (ugh), so I opted for a royal blue fluffy jumper, pink jeans and trusty pink Docs: my go-to emergency outfit.

Sorted.

OK, I wasn't going to be giving Miss World sleepless nights, but it was an improvement on the zombie I'd faced in the mirror earlier. My heart did a little extra thud as I heard a car pull up outside and I went downstairs.

'Late night?' said Toby.

'Very,' I said, fastening my seat belt. 'Is it that obvious?'

He laughed. 'I meant the wedding, as in did it go on for long after I left?' He turned the key in the ignition. 'I've got to meet my dad at half eleven, so sorry it's not more original, but do you want to go for a coffee?'

Yesssss. I'm a coffee vampire at the best of times and on five hours sleep, I'd reached the raging caffeine lust that says, *Hold the water, I'll just chew the beans.* 'Sounds great,' I said.

As soon as we got out of the car he took hold of my hand. When we joined the queue he wrapped his arms around me from behind; kissed the top of my head when he'd given the order. Then once we'd sat down he rested his hand on my knee.

All of this was new and felt good. Very, very good in fact. And if there was a hint of *but you're not Matt* lurking, then the twinkly future thoughts were shining bright enough to mask it.

'So, do you see your dad a lot?' I asked, when we'd settled into the sofa.

He folded his arms and crossed one leg over his knee. 'Hmmm, it's kind of . . .'

I picked up my mug in both hands and blew on the hot coffee to give him a little thinking space.

He uncrossed his legs and sat forward. 'OK. Right. My mum left my dad for Jeff.' He spat the name out like it was covered in mould. No love lost between the pair of them then.

'Jeff's your stepdad?'

More *eeew* face. 'God, no, he's Mum's boyfriend.' He took a slurp of his coffee. 'Mum and Dad split up. Dad had a breakdown and I moved up here with Mum and Jeff.'

And with that, he pulled the shutters down.

In an effort to lift the mood, I blurted out the first thing that popped into my head. 'Do you want to come to an eighteenth party with me in a couple of weeks?'

Oh balls-tastic. I felt my face go Ribena red. Blatantly assuming we'd still *be* 'us' in two weeks. What next, Daisy? Sound him out on honeymoon destinations?

'Love to,' he answered, cool as if I'd asked if he wanted a biscuit with his coffee. 'So tell me about the rest of the wedding,' he continued, with the last trace of sadness fading from his voice. 'Best man try it on with you after I'd gone?'

I laughed, grateful for the topic change, and the conversation flowed from one crazy party story to the next until all the time had been swallowed by easy, no-stress chat.

Too soon we both stood up and he wrapped his arms round me again, and said, 'Thanks for coming out.'

'Fank*ooo*,' I said, face smooshed slightly uncomfortably against his chest.

With Matt, my body had just automatically fit with his. Cosy, familiar. I didn't even have to think, like putting slippers on. I couldn't imagine Toby ever being slippers. So yeah, it might have been a bit awkward, but it was something I was definitely prepared to work on.

Outside and, hmmm, was it my imagination or was the sky bluer than usual? The overcast gloom of earlier had been replaced by some fluffy clouds in the shape of cherubs. The sun was shining more golden. The trees were greener. The flowers . . . flowerier. And were those shiny-plumed birds really chirruping upbeat love songs?

Oh boy. Toby was a human Instagram filter. So *this* was how not being fed up felt. I'd almost forgotten. And the farewell smooch action in the car was highly un-slippers.

'Hope you have a good time with your dad,' I said when I eventually prised myself off him.

He pulled a face. 'I won't, but thanks anyway. See you tomorrow, gorgeous.'

He drove off, leaving me madly grinning, and literally skipping to the front door with joy.

With the rest of the day free I decided to head round to Ayesha's to a) thank her in person for giving me the nudge into Toby's (toned) arms and b) update her on recent developments. I texted straight after he'd dropped me home, but she said she had 'stuff' to sort out and could I leave it till three?

When I arrived at five past, her mum opened the door. 'Hi, Daisy. They're upstairs, go on up.'

They're. Small word, major clue. But I was too dumb to pick up on it. Ayesha's door was ajar, so I pushed it open with a cheery, 'Hiya.'

Oh.

Beth was sitting cross-legged on Ayesha's bed, my surprise mirrored in her expression. She stared at me staring at her and then scratched her nose with one hand, fiddling with a plush Olaf the Snowman with the other.

This was obviously one big set-up.

'Hi, Daisy,' she said eventually.

'Er, hi, Beth,' I said back.

Awkward.

Beth started biting the skin round her thumb, a dead giveaway she was nervous. Ditto my hair-twiddling in the doorway as I hesitated, thinking what to say next. Considering what I'd said to her last time we met, I had to choose carefully. I opened my mouth, hoping the right words would somehow fall out.

They didn't.

Ayesha took charge.

'Right.' She clapped her hands. 'I literally can't go on with the pair of you sulking like babies. You need to sort this out NOW.'

She continued in her best assembly voice. 'Ladies, we have been friends for over five years now. *Five years.* Daisy, Beth, there is nothing, I repeat, *nothing*, more important than our friendship. And yet you two are threatening everything we have.

'I am not exaggerating when I say our friendship is the Gold Standard by which I judge all other relationships in my life. And I for one will not stand by and stay quiet while you two completely disregard our sacred bond over a stupid falling out.'

She lifted a crumpled piece of A3 from her desk and held it up like an ancient scroll. 'The Rules, ladies, the Rules.'

I laughed, stretching out my hand to grab it. 'Is that the original? Let's have a look.'

She moved it out of reach. 'I thought we all needed to be reminded of . . .' she dipped her head to look and pointed at a line: 'Rule number 7: *Boyfriends are the icing, but girlfriends are the cake*. This is the rule that tells us we must never let a boy come between us. So I have brought you here to tell you both, face to face, that I cannot be caught in the middle of this falling out any longer.

'Beth, you need to accept that Daisy was only trying to look out for you. Daisy, you need to respect Beth's choices. The time has come for both of you to make up. Basically, you need to start acting like mature women instead of a . . . a . . . massive pair of tits.'

Seeing the tatty original Rules had done the trick. I looked over at Beth with a pang of sadness. God, I'd been such a bitch. I'd given a snippy argument the legs to run off with our years of friendship and let it get within a whisker of reaching *never speak to each other again*.

Then Beth's shoulders began to shudder. OMG, was she *crying*? I looked helplessly at Ayesha, my concern echoed on her face, and instinctively we both moved towards poor Beth.

As we reached her, Beth let out a gasping howl. 'We're a massive pair of *what*?'

There was a pause. The three of us looked at each other, burst out laughing, and we only stopped when Ayesha's hysterical tears washed one of her contact lenses out and she made us get down on the carpet to look for it.

By the time I could speak again, my stomach muscles were aching like I'd done twenty-four hours of sit-ups.

'I am sorry, Beth,' I said when we were calmer. 'For, you know, calling Shaney names.'

'He's actually amazing, you know. Even Dad's stopped hating him,' she said with the glassy-eyed passion of the newly brainwashed. But I was channelling the Rules now, in particular #2: *Always support your friends.*

'He must be doing something right,' I said. 'I've never seen you this happy.'

'Well, I suppose you were only looking out for me,' she admitted. 'And sorry for calling you bitter and heartless and going on about Matt. That was out of order.'

'Halle-flaming-lujah!' Ayesha did prayer hands and looked up to the ceiling. 'The two of you have been driving me mad. Now, hug.'

Me and Beth obliged, and it felt good to have my friend back.

I wanted Beth to know I really meant this. 'We'll have to get the boys together,' I said, 'so I can meet Shaney.'

'And I hear I need to meet a certain someone too,'

said Beth. 'We should all go see a film or something.'

My phone buzzed in my pocket and I raised both eyebrows at the girls. Speak of the Devil and he dialeth your number.

'Toby. Hi.'

I could only just hear above the traffic noise. 'Hi yourself. Where are you?'

'With my friends. At Ayesha's.'

Kissy kissy went the so-called friends. '*You massive pair of tits*', I mouthed.

'Do you want me to come and give you a lift home?' he said loudly. 'I've just dropped my dad at the train station.'

I looked at Ayesha and Beth. 'No, it's OK, thanks.' There was still work to be done here. I wasn't ready to leave yet.

But he can't have heard me. 'What's your mate's postcode? I can be with you in ten minutes,' he yelled.

'I was planning on staying longer really,' I said.

'It'll have to be now; I've got to get to rugby by four thirty.'

'Doesn't matter then,' I said. 'I'm fine walking, honest. Thanks though.'

'Right.' And there was a pause.

'So, see you tomorrow?' I tried, sending psychic *not being ungrateful* vibes.

'Tell you what,' he said, 'take a selfie with your mates and send me that instead.'

'A selfie?' I laughed. 'What for?'

'So I can see your beautiful face of course.'

'Aw shucks,' I said and covered the phone.

'He wants a photo of us,' I whispered and gestured at the girls to come closer. I reached out to put an arm round each of them. Beth took the phone and stretched out her arm.

Cheeeeese.

'You still there, Toby?' I said when Beth handed it back.

'Yep. Have you done it?'

'Sending it now.' I tapped the touch screen and whooshed it off to him. A beep and then a laugh came back down the line.

'Who's who?'

'Ayesha, dark hair, Beth tongue out and me big hair,' I answered.

'Love it!' he said. 'Call you later.'

'Send me that photo,' said Ayesha.

'And me,' said Beth, grabbing the phone to have a

look. 'So come on, what's he like, this Toby?'

'Let's see,' said Ayesha. 'What would you get if you crossed a Greek god, a movie star and the hottest man on earth?' She mock swooned across the bed.

'Oooh,' said Beth. 'I would get very excited. How come he wanted a selfie?'

'Dunno. He's always asking for them. I took one with my nana the other day.'

'Really?' laughed Beth. 'Has he got a nan fetish or something? Does he get you to dress up in cardigans and a cauliflower perm wig?'

'He's a nice person,' I said, shoving her. '*Very* nice. Not like you.'

'Do you think it might get to be serious?' asked Ayesha.

'No!' I said. 'Well, maybe. I don't know.'

And along with my happy friend feelings, that's the question that filled my head as I walked home late.

Would it?

And, more importantly, did I want it to?

CHAPTER 11

Rubbing my eyes and yawning, I nudged the door of the sociology classroom open with my boot and ambled in. Badger, insanely cheerful for 9 o'clock on a drizzly Monday morning, had pulled out the seat next to his and was waving me over. 'Daisy! Thank you so much, I had the best time yesterday.'

Eh? Then I twigged: 'Oh right, the audition. How'd it go?'

'Amazing.' Bless him, he looked so happy. 'Harv said my brass was exactly the edge the band needs.'

Obviously, I wasn't at the audition and Marv 'n' Harv were the experts, but *edgy?* Badger was as sweet as a gingerbread house stuffed with kittens, but he had the 'edginess' of a custard cream.

'Hello, Brittany,' Badger said cheerily as Little Miss

Nasty breezed in. 'Did you have a good weekend?'

She had her head dipped to her phone, making a beeline for the only available seat which, as fate would have it, was next to me. *Ace.*

'Yep,' she said, without taking her eyes from the screen. 'I did.'

'Do anything exciting?'

Nothing, not even a grunt in reply. How rude! She just cast him a brief warthog-chewing-on-a-jellyfish glance before resuming her tap-tap-tapping.

It was high time that girl booked herself in for a personality MOT. She may have been above averagely pretty and from Texas, and so slightly exotic, but that was no excuse for her off-the-scale rudeness to lovely Badger. Or to me, for that matter, thinking back to that first tutorial. Brittany was clearly a girl whose version of the Rules was very different from mine.

The teacher walked in, weighed down with books and worksheets.

'Morning, everyone,' she said, handing stuff out. '*Riiiight*, so we're still looking at societal changes brought about by war. I want you to answer the questions together using what we covered last week. Pairs or on your own, it's up to you.'

To my left, I heard soft beeping and glanced down. Brittany was typing 'societal changes + war' into Google.

'That's cheating!' I hissed.

'No, that's initiative,' she snapped back. She started making notes on the pad on her desk and the mild irk I'd been experiencing was suddenly not quite so mild. In fact, it was hard-core irk and I knew if she did one more vexing thing in my presence, my irate gob would –

The door creaked open and my irk was temporarily distracted.

A floral forest with legs entered, bringing with it a waft of nose-pleasing sweetness. As the huge bouquet passed the teacher's desk, Brittany *squeeeed* (decibel level: mass piglet castration) and I felt a spike in my irritation levels. Of course, she'd assume any romcom-esque gesture was for her. And that she'd *always* be the girl who got a guy in jeans and hipster trainers, his no-doubt cutie face hidden behind all those blooms.

'Ohmygoshohmygosh!' squeaked Brittany, reaching out her arms.

I recognise those trainers, I thought.

'Sorry for the interruption, people,' Toby said. 'Daisy, these are for you.' And he laid the flowers on my desk.

!!!!!!!!!!!!

All credit to her, Brittany styled it out with an instant eye roll and *whatever* expression that was quite unlike my own gasping guppy impression.

'Th-thanks,' I stuttered.

'You're welcome. Call you later,' he said. Then with a general 'Sorry' to the class, he strolled back out.

With Toby gone, the spell was broken and the teacher returned to her senses. 'OK, thank you, everyone. Let's get back to work. And Daisy, they're very nice, but could you put them out of the way, please.'

I placed the flowers on the windowsill behind me, tucking the cellophane in carefully to protect them. I unstuck the little white envelope and, fighting the urge to rip it open, stashed it in my bag.

I tried to get back into the session. Discussing women's role in wartime could not be further up my intellectual alley and usually I'd be elbowing my way to the front of any debate, but poor Badger ended up doing most of the work. Between the *Alice in Wonderland* 'Read Me' message radiating from the envelope and the waves of hate from Brittany, my head was all over the place.

Those spider-lashed baby blues raked my face with a jealous glare. Oh ho ho. *Someone* obviously had the hots for Toby. Interesting. Now, as a rule, gloat didn't float my boat, but for getting one over on Brittany I was prepared to make an exception. The gorgeous bouquet was proof karma existed and it was definitely rooting for Badger and me.

But satisfying as teaching Brittany a lesson felt, the real burning issue was what had I done to deserve these flowers? I was metaphorically aflame with curiosity.

Finally, the lesson finished and I was free. Badger went off to music and Brittany flounced off to I-don't-care-where. And then, oh joy, we were alone at last: me and my organic, responsibly grown blooms *d'amour*.

I carried them down the back stairs to the library, installed myself in a corner booth and then – at last! – got my sweaty little mitts on the envelope. Inside was a postcard of a daisy. Cute. I turned it over:

Thanks for a great weekend. Txx

OK, maybe it wasn't exactly a sonnet, but it was enough to put a smile on my face.

'You like the flowers then?' Toby had snuck up from nowhere and was pulling up a chair. 'I hope the teacher didn't mind.'

'No,' I said, soppy grin growing. 'It was fine. And they're beautiful, thank you so much.'

'You're welcome,' he said, with a smile to match my own. 'I wanted to say sorry.'

I smiled some more. 'I'm not sure what for.'

'For not staying longer at the wedding, then having to run off to meet my dad yesterday.'

'Oh, don't worry about the wedding,' I said. 'Or any of it. It was just nice to see you. How did it go with your dad?'

He shrugged, fiddling with the ribbon on the bouquet. 'Let's just say I've seen him better.'

That didn't sound promising. 'Has he gone back down south now?'

'Yeah, he never stays long. And he was OK, apart from the usual paranoid crap about Mum and Jeff. I just ignore him when he starts now. Anyway,' he screeched his chair up until our knees were touching, 'the flowers are only half of it. What I really wanted to give you is this.'

He put his hands to my face and drew me into a kiss. A lovely loooong kiss. A lovely, long kiss that went on . . . and on. And then on some more.

Which was obviously nice, but, well, public snogathons, even with Hottie McHotlips here, got me more fidgety and embarrassed than frisky.

Especially if a stranger shouted, 'Get a room!'

And people started laughing.

And a member of staff heard them.

I opened one eye to peep over Toby's shoulder. Wah!

I unglued myself from Toby's lovely lips to whisper, 'The librarian's coming over.'

But it was too late: he was right here, right now, and he didn't look happy.

'This is a *library*,' he hissed, face like a thundercloud and with a beetling monobrow. 'I can't believe what I'm seeing.'

Toby did a mock double take at the shelves. 'Oh, it's a *library*. Well, that explains the books . . .' He squinted at the man's name badge. 'Colin.'

That whole alpha-male crap thing Toby was trying would normally have wound me up, but the librarian's outrage was so OTT I couldn't help letting rip with a snorty *ha ha ha*.

Oops.

Colin's face was a picture.

A picture of a man giving birth to a hedgehog to be exact.

'This behaviour is totally unacceptable!' he said. And as his eye rugs vigorously twerked, I laughed so hard I almost had a wee on the carpet.

Toby was struggling to keep a straight face too. 'Sorry, what was that?'

'Get. Out. Now,' spluttered Colin. 'I'm reporting you if you don't leave.'

'Daisy, I've got to go now anyway,' Toby said ultra-calmly. 'But I'll see you later, OK?' Then with a cheery, 'Bye, Colin,' he strolled off.

No kidding, the door hadn't even swung shut before the librarian turned on me. 'Student card,' he snapped, holding out his hand.

'What for?'

'Student card. Now.' And he *clicked his fingers in front of my nose*! With a simultaneous *click*, my self-control switched itself off.

'I forgot to bring it,' I lied.

'Then you'll have to come to the Principal's office with me.' And as he leaned in close, *ugh!* I saw globs of white gunk had collected in the corners of his lips. I didn't know whether to hand him a tissue or spew on his shoes.

'Why?' I protested. 'I haven't done anything wrong. Except laugh. Sorry for laughing.'

He jabbed at a sign behind me: *This is a workspace, not*

a social space. 'Can you read that?' he said.

Through some supreme effort of will, I didn't bash the patronising git with my beautiful begonias. Instead I shouldered my rucksack and made a move towards the door, clutching my flowers.

But Colin wasn't through with me yet. 'I said, tell me what the sign says.'

A hail of spit landed on my face. *Barf.* And when he stepped forward to block my path, something snapped. The rational part of my brain was telling me to say sorry and get my ass out of there, but a trace of Toby's up-yours attitude lingered, mixed with flashbacks to Mr Fox. Because instead of meekly parroting what was on the sign, I opened my mouth and slowly and deliberately said, 'Get a life, Colin.'

Then I legged it. Naughty, naughty Daisy.

What did the prospectus say again: *Our staff treat students as adults?* Hmmm. Looked like it was Colin who couldn't read.

I hadn't even got down the corridor before my rebel self sloped off, leaving me with a sneaky sick feeling. I knew there was no way Colin would let me get away with this.

Thank God for Toby, I thought. He was the only decent

thing about this place. Well, apart from Badger. And the clean toilets. And the catering wasn't too bad either.

But still.

I went to the canteen where I guessed Toby would be waiting. Outside, the rain pelted on the skylights, giving the place a trapped-in-the-drum-of-a-washing-machine ambience. Condensation was running down the walls and the air was thick with the smell of Lynx and boyfeet. And talk about loud. I had the urge to put my hands over my ears as I fought through the crowd, a lone salmon swimming upstream.

There was Toby. A tall, rugby-shaped figure flipping back his mop of hair as he squeezed into Rugby Corner, hands braced on the table to sit down. I'd got as far as the information point halfway along the wall and lifted my arm to wave when —

What was *this*?

Brittany had flung both arms round him and latched herself on to his face. Her silky ombre-tinted hair rippled to the beat of her bobbing head. Was she fishing a foreign object out with her tongue? As I stared, her hands moved up to clutch the back of his head. Maybe she was feasting on his soul. Or maybe I'd just got Toby all wrong.

First Matt and Rosa. Now Toby and Brittany.

I'd practically shattered my elbow on a chair turning for the exit when I realised Brittany had unhooked herself. And the relief nearly rubberised my leg bones as I saw her victim's face:

NOT Toby.

Very similar from a distance, but crucially *not* him. Her snog-buddy was a slightly less symmetrical, slightly less flawless almost-Toby. The Primark to Toby's Armani, if you will.

I hung about, wobbly with relief and cradling my flowers in my arms. But when he hadn't arrived after five minutes I went off to find a quiet spot to wait for next lesson.

Why was I wobbly? Because . . . well, I wasn't in love with Toby. But I *was* in like. A whole sparkly heap of getting-over-Matt in like.

And I don't think I realised how much until I thought Brittany had him.

I'd promised Badger I'd come and watch his first proper rehearsal with the band after college. Driving over, Mum had told me he'd need to work his socks off to learn the set for the next wedding and maybe it was too much to ask. But it only took a few notes before even stone-tone-deaf me realised he was majorly talented. And man alive! Where was the timid creature from college? He owned the tiny studio stage with Glastonbury headliner strutability.

With barely a glance at the sheet music Harv gave him, he was soon swapping the trumpet for a couple of similar shiny things (flumpet? strumpet?) he'd brought along.

Incredible. I reached for my phone to film him, then cursed myself as I realised I'd left it at home. As they ran through the set, it was obvious Harv was right: Badger was Something Blue's missing edge.

Who'd have thought under that geeky *Star Trek: The Next Generation* T-shirt beat the heart of a natural-born showman? And Mum's gorgeous voice sounded sweeter than ever with the brass behind it. Genuine spine tingles time.

They played a forty minute set pretty much straight through and when the final note died I stood *awoooooo*-ing and air-punching while Badger blushed and bowed simultaneously. Then, wiping his palms down Captain Jean-Luc Picard's face, he walked over to where I was still clapping.

'Was that OK?' he said twisting his fingers round.

'OK? Totally mind-blowing more like,' I said with a grin.

'He's fantastic, isn't he?' said Harv. Marv and Mum murmured in agreement. Badger beamed and Jean-Luc's pointy slaphead swelled with pride.

Harv handed Badger a card. 'Obviously, we'll have a few more practice runs this week, but in case I forget the address and directions to the venue on Saturday are on here. Six o'clock start.'

'Affirmative, Captain,' said Badger with a mock salute.

'Be there or be rhomboid,' chipped in Marv.

'Make it so,' said Harv with a forward hand movement and the three of them *heh-heh-heh-ed* in unison. Yep, they were definitely geeks of a feather and it was a total stroke of genius getting them together, if I did say so myself. Go me.

Mum drove us home and as soon as we got there I raced up the stairs to retrieve my phone from where it was blinking away on my dressing table. And how many times had Toby rung? FIVE. Yes, FIVE. Cue big-style warm and fuzzies: who'd have thought the King of Cool was actually the King of Keen?

Oh ye-aah, oh ye-aah. I had a brief, happy body pop in front of the mirror while I called him back. Check me out: five phone calls! In the space of, what? Two hours? He must —

'Hello.'

Was it my imagination or was his 'Hello' a trifle frosty?

Well, I got that. It was annoying to keep calling someone and get no reply. 'Sorry, I left my phone at home,' I explained. 'How are you?'

'Where've you been?' he said.

Maybe his abruptness was the reason I started waffling on about *Badger's epic talent* this and *Badger's stage act* that and *Badger's the best thing since they supersized Jaffa Cakes* the other. Whatever it was, when Toby interrupted me with, 'What, that geek from tutorial?' it knocked me right off my stride again.

I laughed. 'Well, yeah, he's in tutorial and he does have some nerdy qualities, I suppose. But he's dead sweet and *sooo* talented.'

Silence. Followed by more silence.

'I looked for you at break,' I said, not really getting what was going on. 'In the canteen.'

'Right.'

I waited for him to expand, but nope.

'Is something up?' I asked.

'Like what?'

'Is it your dad?'

'My *dad*?' he said, incredulous. 'What's my dad got to do with anything?'

'Um, I don't know.' I was so confused now.

'So,' he said, flat-voiced, 'when are you seeing him again?'

'Your dad?'

'No! Trumpet boy!'

Aha. Toby hadn't just got hold of the wrong *end* of the stick, he'd grabbed the wrong stick altogether.

'Toby, do you think there's something going on with me and Badger?'

'Well, is there?'

'Don't be daft!' I protested. 'I'll see him on Saturday at the wedding and probably at college before then, but otherwise, no.'

I could almost hear the thoughts slotting into place. *Band. Daisy. Badger. Me. College.*

'*Okaaaay*,' he said eventually. 'But you understand where I'm coming from, yeah?'

'Erm . . .' I said.

'*You* wouldn't like it, would you?'

Would I have been happy with Matt bigging up another

girl? 'Probably not.' I admitted. 'Sorry.'

'It's OK.' He sighed. 'Forget it. This eighteenth you want me to go to, when is it again?'

Normal Toby was back for the rest of the call, but even as we chatted about Tom's party, there was an itch in the back of my mind. Where the hell did that Badger business come from?

'Daisy?'

I tuned back in. 'Sorry, yes?'

'Wedding, Saturday. Why don't I help you out?'

'Wow,' I said. I hadn't seen that coming. 'Are you sure?'

'Yeah. I mean, I've got a rugby match in the afternoon, but I could come for the evening do. Didn't you say you were short-handed?'

With that, he was lovely again.

'And,' he continued, his voice lower, 'you know I only said that about Trumpet Boy because I care, don't you?'

'Er . . .' I said, my heart suddenly pounding in my ears. 'Um, thanks.'

'I mean it,' he said. 'If I wasn't bothered, I wouldn't have said anything. And how are the flowers? Did you get them home OK on the bus?'

'They're beautiful,' I said, glancing at the vase containing proof he cared. 'Thank you.'

'You're welcome,' he said. 'So I'll see you tomorrow at break in the canteen, yeah?'

As we squeaked our goodbyes (well, mine was a squeak), 'because I care' was bouncing round my head.

I hugged Toby's words close as I peeled every photo of Matt off my bedroom wall. Then I unpinned three years' worth of Valentines, Christmas and birthday cards from the corkboard by my mirror and stuffed the lot in my desk drawer, out of sight.

I was moving on.

CHAPTER 12

Well, top marks to Detective Colin for tracking me down so swiftly. He must've been on the college system, trawling through the student mugshots within a nanosecond of my leaving the library the day before. Clearly, this was a man who believed revenge was a dish best served piping hot from the microwave.

I'd checked my college email first thing and there it was, a date with fate, scheduled for nine o'clock. Me, the Vice Principal and a no-doubt almighty rollicking.

At least the bus was on time, giving me a fifteen-minute window to raid the vending machine for the sugar rush required to help me woman up for the showdown, and go to the loo.

Oh joy unparalleled.

Human Bratz doll Brittany was in there, laminating her face with further layers of beige. *Of course* she was. And dressed in spangly hot pants and a crop top, as though she might at any moment be asked to dance round a football pitch. Or a pole.

She paused mid-trowel and stared at me in the mirror as I snuck past behind her.

'Debbie, I hear you're dating Toby Smith, right?'

Two thoughts here: a) you know my name, cow-features, and b) I suppose I am.

I grunted a non-answer and scuttled to the furthest cubicle. There was no time for this: I had urgent bathroom fireworks to deal with. Yesterday, I was Ms Badass-tude. Today, Ms I-am-screwed and, as crap o'clock approached, my insides were churning.

I'd had my share of grief with Mr Fox, but never a summons from the Head at St Mary's, and judging by my quivering intestines, I wasn't a natural-born rebel.

When I emerged, Brittany had gone and I did a quick reflection check, trying to draw courage from my fifties vibe. Reapplied the ruby pout, smoothed my hair and straightened my hoop earrings. Counted to ten . . . and I was off to confront the dragon in his lair.

'I'm here to see the Vice Principal,' I said to the man on the desk. 'Daisy Green.'

He held up a finger and buzzed. 'Student here for you, Mr Snape.'

Snape. I hoped that wasn't a Bad Omen.

Furball Colin was already there, almost incontinent with excitement as he hopped from foot to foot. Ace. I might have failed my maths GCSE, but five years with Mr Fox had given me excellent teacher-blanking skills. So while Snape blah-ed on about respect and not making the best start to my time in college, I was able to just nod contritely until it was Colin's turn to play the war-movie baddie.

Him: 'Tell me the name of the boy you were with.'

Me: 'What boy?'

Him: (*eye twitching*) 'You know very well what boy. The one you were talking to in the library.'

Me: 'I don't know his name.'

Him: (*yelling*) 'Ve have vays of making you talk!'

Then he strapped me to the chair, mwahahah-ing as he twirled his monobrow like a movie villain's moustache.

Or at least I'm sure that's what would've happened had Snape not stepped in with a timely, 'Thank you

Colin. I'll take it from here.'

'Well, young lady,' Snape continued after Colin had stalked out, 'don't think that means there are no consequences.'

He handed me a two-week library ASBO along with an invitation (aka threat) to 'engage' my parents in a 'dialogue' should other such 'behaviour' occur.

By this point, my inner rebel was desperate to 'engage' in a short 'dialogue' of my own regarding Colin's 'behaviour'. (Two words. Second word: off.) But because my brain contained a molecule of sense, I shut up, leaving the office with my ego bashed, but my college place intact. For the time being at least.

A verbal slap round the chops from Professor Snape wasn't the ideal start to the day and I hoped it wouldn't get any worse. No such luck.

I raced up to maths just in time to hear the dreaded words 'Test' and 'Next week'. There were other words filling the spaces in between, but they didn't catch my attention.

I wished I hadn't bothered racing. If there was one thing I hated more than a maths test it was . . . actually nothing. There was *nothing* I hated more than a maths test.

Scheissenburgers.

Every minute of that maths lesson mysteriously stretched to an hour and it was only the thought of meeting Toby in the canteen at the end that kept me going.

'Everyone, this is Daisy,' said Toby when break finally arrived. 'Shift up and let her in.'

'Hi,' I said, damping down the nerves. Now no one would ever refer to me as petite, but crowded on a canteen bench with the giants of the college rugby team, I almost disappeared.

'Daisy, this is Jozz, Mozz, Bozz and Tozz,' he (possibly) said, gesturing round the identikit group. You could've replaced any one of them with a donkey wearing an 'I'm a rugby lad' hat and even their own mothers wouldn't be able to tell the difference.

Various vague 'hiyas' came back, but then everyone (Toby included) re-engaged with the conversation I'd just interrupted: a post-mortem of a night out I hadn't been on, to a club I'd never heard of with a crowd of people I didn't know. And all accompanied by unfunny you-had-to-be-there in-jokes, while I shrank a little further into the seat. I hadn't felt this out of place since Beth dragged me along to VikingStock with Stinky Pete.

Not one of them spoke to me. I'd crash-landed on an alien planet where sexist entities mimicked humans and, as the banter got dodgier and more raucous, I zoned out. It was possible that individually some of them might have been reasonable lads, who respected women and had actual conversations, but in herd form they were just hee-hawing donkeys.

I was idly pondering whether to use my powers of invisibility for good or evil when — *yay, supreme* — Brittany sashayed over. She treated me to an exaggerated *What? You? Here?* double take before hitching herself onto the knee of the Toby-alike she'd been face-munching earlier. Mozz? Bozz? Turned out to be Jozz. Head donkey.

Toby had his arm round me, squeezing me close while he carried on chipping in to the 'legendary' tale of the beer-n-birds marathon Jozz was braying about. Hands clasped round his neck, Brittany giggled along; a cliché hidden in a stereotype wrapped up in *hang your head in shame, woman*.

After what seemed like hours, Jozz concluded his snoresome tale with, 'And then the next morning I told her, 'They don't call it Bag a Slag night for nothing, love.'

Charming.

'*Hee-haw-hee-haw*,' hee-hawed the lads.

'What did she say to that?' asked Random Other.

'Nothing,' shrugged Jozz. 'She just started crying and told me to get out of her house.'

'Those were the days, eh Jozzer?' said A Different One, play-punching him in the arm. 'Can't do that now you're a married man.'

Toby nudged me with his shoulder, squeezing my hand in a secret *what an utter moron* gesture (I hoped). But he still brayed along.

As did Brittany, while close by a century of feminism smacked its head against the wall.

In a parallel world somewhere, Daisy the Sexism Slayer was gunning Jozz down in a series of killer comebacks. *Zap! This is for womankind. Boff! We do not use the S-word. Bash! We do not make girls cry. Kapow!* But in dimension Here and Now, surrounded by Toby's bonehead buddies, I was mute.

Next lesson finally came and the crowd thinned, meaning I could escape without drawing attention to myself.

'Hey,' said Toby. Still holding my hand, he pulled me back down. 'I thought you were on a free. Where are you off to? Library?'

'Ah, *nooo*,' I said and told him the tale of my trip to Room 101 with Snape and Colin.

Toby raised his eyebrows. 'You're barred because of what I said to that loser?'

'Well, no,' I said. 'It was for telling him he needed to get a life after you'd gone.'

Mwah! He planted a smacker on my lips, laughing. 'You nailed it there. *Librarian*. What kind of job is that for a man?'

Completely *not* what I was getting at. Librarians equalled libraries and libraries equalled lovely books you could take home FOR FREE. Duh. Plus, the library really wasn't the place for a snogfest, so Colin was kind of justified in intervening, even if he did go about it the wrong way.

But when I tried explaining this to Toby, he looked at me as if I'd started speaking in tongues.

'He's a freak,' he said, dismissing one subject and starting another with a shrug. 'So, what you doing tonight?'

'Going to footie training with Ayesha.'

He twirled a strand of my hair round his fingers. 'You do see a lot of her, don't you?'

'Not as much as I used to. You know it's her

boyfriend's eighteenth you're coming to?' I smiled. 'Well, if you still want to.'

'Of course I still want to,' he said and put his arms round me. 'You think I'd let you go to a party on your own with all those lads trying it on with you?'

Those words, whispered into my hair as he held me tight, sent tingles right through me. After months of feeling unloved and unwanted, I was glowing inside. He cares! I matter! I'm special!

And the ache of missing Matt started to fade a tiny bit more.

CHAPTER 13

Pinning a hem, eating an apple, getting River ready to go to Nana's and de-stressing a hyper bride on the phone? All in a day's work for Supermum. She was like that blue Indian goddess with a million arms. Except not blue. Or Indian. But she was a multitasking goddess nonetheless.

And me? Well, because Toby was joining Team Something Borrowed later, the day had started with a sparkle. What to wear? Hair definitely down – that was a no-brainer. The teal silk dress with the sequinned peacock then. No glitter nails, no snog-stopping red lips and no false eyelashes. (Well, maybe just the one pair.) Had an excited text from Badger and a can't-wait-to-see-you one from Toby that had me smiling inside and out.

Over the last few days, without either of us saying

anything about it, me and Toby had drifted into spending our free time at college together. When I didn't have a lesson, I'd find him sitting in the canteen, sometimes on his own, mostly with one or two mates or Jozz and Brittany. I'd had a bunch of surprise flowers left on the doorstep and he'd even turned up out of the blue to watch footie training and then driven me and Ayesha home. Dodgy donkey mates aside, the guy could not have been ticking more boxes on the Potential Boyfriend Wish List.

And now he'd volunteered to help at the wedding. And boy, did we need it. This was a BIG DEAL for Something Borrowed. The caterers had sorted out all the waiting staff and the venue had their own in-house team too, but with 150 or so guests there was still loads for us to do.

I was loving the venue: a sculpture gallery which had Dad giddy as a snap-happy kipper. We'd got there first thing to add the finishing touches to the 'Ironic Chandelier Room' (actual name). Thousands of reflective crystal drops dangling off a tier of bicycle wheels to create a chandelier that blinged the room like a disco ball and glinted off the centrepieces. It was a nice nod to the cycle-mad couple's hobby of choice, plus the perfect backdrop for Dad to take some dazzlingly original photos of the dazzlingly gorgeous couple.

Put some people in a wedding environment and they go all Downton Abbey on you. It's *servant do this, servant do that* till you're a gnat's whisker from telling Lord and Lady Bossyboots where to stick their silver service. But as well as being a lovely couple, Megan and Ben had some seriously lovely friends.

Like Rich the Best Man. He was standing near me during the cocktail hour when I realised the waiting staff had moved some of the place cards. Massive panic. I had to sort two table's worth literally minutes before everyone was due to sit down.

'Can I help?' he said discreetly as I fanned the cards out on a table

'That would be great,' I said wholeheartedly. 'I think we must have duplicated some?'

'Allow me.' He consulted my photocopy of the seating plan. 'He's this one here, and he's here and that one is . . . here.'

'Three people with that name,' I said. 'Unbelievable.'

'That's the problem with Guses,' he said with a wink. 'You don't see one for years, then three turn up at once.' I laughed, and a moment later the gong sounded for dinner.

Except it wasn't a gong, it was synchronised bicycle bells the waiting staff had been given. Another of Mum's quirky details that had the guests smiling as they took their seats. I held my breath until it was clear everyone was at the right table.

Disaster averted, things were shaping up to be flawless. Mum's personal touches were everywhere, with Message in a Bottle my favourite. She'd set a big winemaking demijohn up on a table, along with a stack of hand-cut paper hearts and instructions to: 1. Write a wedding message, 2. Roll it up, 3. Stick it in. Then Dad would use them as captions for the online album. Sweet with a capital C.U.T.E.

Bang on seven, Toby arrived, buff and pumped from a 'legendary' rugby win and, in his suit, looking like every Hollywood heartthrob ever rolled into one. As he headed towards me, I went distinctly weak in the knee zone and had to grab the back of a chair.

Dad was all smiles, straight in to shake his hand. 'Toby, thank you so much. We really appreciate the help.'

'You're welcome, Mr Green,' said Toby.

'Call me Nick,' said Dad.

'And I'm Susie,' chipped in Mum, coming up behind us. 'Nice to meet you, Toby.'

In the grand scheme of meet the parents, this was about as smooth as you could ask for and as we started work I was in a rosy cocoon of happy.

'Right then,' Toby said, taking in the room. 'Tell me what you want me to do.'

The guests had only just finished the starters, so apart from Dad's roving snap attacks, it was the lull before the storm for us.

Dad checked his watch. 'Maybe see if the band need a hand with anything?'

'Follow me,' I said, leading Toby to the backstage room.

'Daisy! Hi!' said an incredibly excited Badger as I poked my head round the door, 'I am so nervous about the . . .'

He tailed off as Toby came in behind me.

'All right, mate,' said Toby.

'Er, hello,' said Badger, blinking at him.

'Don't be nervous,' I said. 'You're going to blow them away.'

'Hope so.' He frowned and interlaced his fingers. 'I don't want to let anyone down.'

'Do you need anything?' I asked.

'Um, don't think so,' Badger answered, peering

round the room. He pointed over at a pile of black cases on the floor. 'Got my gear, and Marv and Harv have finished setting up theirs.'

Bless him, he looked terrified. Badger blew out his cheeks, and huff-puff-puffed the air out. 'Warm-ups,' he explained.

Toby turned to leave, but before I followed, I hurried over to Badger and impulsively gave him a hug. 'Don't worry, you're going to be amazing.'

Toby stepped forward and grabbed my hand. 'Come *on*!'

'Ow!' I half winced, half laughed as he pulled me out through the door. He immediately let go and I wiggled my fingers while he swerved round a waiter carrying a tray piled high with roast beef

'Toby?' I said. 'What's the rush?'

He didn't so much as glance back. 'No rush,' I heard him say.

As I caught up with him at the far wall, Dad popped up. 'Can you man the booth now?'

'No problem, Nick,' said Toby. 'We're on it, aren't we, Daisy?'

'Great,' said Dad and waggled his camera. 'Just off to get a few more casual ones.'

'Toby,' I said when Dad had gone. 'That hurt.'

'Did it?' He picked up my hand, turning it over to kiss my fingers. 'I guess I don't know my own strength.'

Now he was looking over my shoulder and when I turned my head I saw Badger chatting with mucho enthusiasm to a girl by the stage. She was one of the guests but she looked kind of familiar. Before I could work out where I knew her from, Toby pulled my arm around his waist. 'Tell me how we do the photo booth.'

I took him over and went through the set-up. Costumes were in the wicker hamper, the madder the combination, the better. The guests chose what they fancied, then stood in front of the backdrop. With the camera fixed on a tripod it was a doddle to use the red velvet curtains to frame the picture, vintage cinema style. Then *click* and on to the next in line.

'Dead easy,' I said.

I looked up and caught the eye of Badger's lady friend who gave me a little wave.

'Ohhh, she goes to college, doesn't she?' I said to Toby. 'That girl in the amazing purple feathery hat thing. I've seen her in the library.'

He peered over, shrugged. 'No idea. Maybe.'

But it was definitely her and as she went to sit back

down I waved Badger over to where Toby and I were standing.

'Is everything OK?' he said hesitantly.

'Who's your friend? She's at college, isn't she?'

His expression told me *I've got the big fat hots for her* without his lips needing to move.

'Gem-Gemma,' he replied as every drop of blood in his body migrated to his face. 'We get the same bus. The groom's her cousin.'

'I think you're in there, mate,' said Toby, suddenly clapping a surprised-looking Badger on the back. Surprised Gemma might fancy him or surprised Toby was being friendly? No idea.

We were interrupted by Best Man Rich dinging on a bicycle bell. He'd obviously had a cheeky sherbet or five and as he swayed to his feet my cringe sensors started twitching: *Please please please don't wreck this beautiful wedding.*

And he didn't. I saw Dad's shoulders de-tense as he began panning the video camera round to catch the guests' reactions to the speech. Nope, nothing crude, rude or lewd was coming out of the best man's mouth, just the sweet story of a couple who'd met at school.

'To paraphrase the Bard,' Rich said, shiny face

beaming, 'the course of true love never ran smoothly and is strewn with air miles. When Ben spent two years working in Australia it was tough, but they showed us all that if you truly belong together, distance doesn't matter. Ladies and gentlemen, Megan and Ben!' finished Rich, his voice cracking as he toasted the happy couple.

I clapped and held an imaginary champagne flute up, but his words had struck a major chord: long-distance relationships aren't always doomed.

In an alternative dimension, un-knee jerk me was back in the yard at St Mary's hearing, *I'm sorry Daisy, I'm going to Spain*. And this other-me was experiencing the same body-shaking *What?* But instead of immediately spitting out an ultimatum, she was saying, *I understand you want to help your mum. Don't worry, we can make it work.*

Through my head, a rapid montage of *could've-been* scenes played out. Matt sweeping me into a hug at Arrivals; Matt and me drinking cocktails on the beach; Matt and me lazing in a hammock; Matt coming back once the bar was on its feet . . .

Then with a *snap!* the *could've beens* were back to being *never will bes*. Toby was clicking his fingers in front of my nose.

'Earth calling Daisy,' he said. 'Come in, Daisy. Planet Wedding needs you.'

'Sorry,' I said, shaking my head slightly, 'I was miles away.'

Something Blue were onstage now and I smiled to see no trace of Badger's nerves as the band made the transition from the romantic first dance ballad to the upbeat tunes designed to lure people on to the dance floor. Within minutes the photo booth was all hectic plastic palm trees and feather boas a gogo.

As I worked, I kept glancing over at Toby who certainly looked like he was having a great time. He was an absolute natural at flirting with the women, being jokey with the men and I relaxed, falling into the rhythm of costume, pose, photo.

Following the success of his speech, Best Man Rich had his banter cannons on full blast, coaxing and herding until pretty much every member of the party had gurned under the weight of a pair of giant sunnies and a policeman's helmet. He lurched over to me, glowing with joy (or cheeky sherbets) and still wearing the illuminated fairy wings he'd taken a shine to earlier.

'You're doing a great job. Brilliant. Best wedding

ever.' He put his arm round me and squeezed, kissing me on the cheek. 'I mean it. It's fantastico.'

I laughed. Nearby, Toby was unbuckling the chinstrap on a unicorn horn and mane set. His eyes flicked our way and even in the dim light I could tell he was annoyed.

'You know,' Rich beamed, still with one arm slung round my waist, 'I've known Meg and Ben since school and even then I knew that one day I'd be going to their wedding. You can just tell, can't you? You see these two people and you can't imagine how one could exist without the other. Like Ant and Dec. I remember one time –'

Then suddenly Toby was in front of us. And he wasn't annoyed, he was *furious*.

Merrily oblivious to Toby's grim expression, Rich waved his wand in tipsy greeting. 'All right, mate? I was just saying that everything today has been amaz–'

'Get off.' Toby's tone was neutral, but not the words.

'Do what?' Rich answered, looking puzzled.

'Stop. Groping. Her,' said Toby.

Rich glanced down at his arm and blinked, as if seeing it for the first time. 'Oh, right. Sorry, Daisy, erm, mate.'

He untangled himself from around my waist and stood there unsteadily for a few seconds, as if unsure what to do next. Toby was silent. I was speechless. With a hesitant wave, Rich was soon just a pair of flashing fairy wings swallowed up by the dance floor.

Toby watched him walk away, then turned to me. '*Why?*' He said.

'What?'

'Why do girls have to flirt all the time?' He spoke in a low voice, while plucking at some imaginary thread on his sleeve.

'We don't! *I* don't!'

'Daisy, I *saw* you.'

I opened my mouth, but he just kept going. 'See those girls there?' He waved over at the queue. 'Every single one of them has been eyeing me up all night. Some of them have been back FIVE times for photos. And do you know why I don't do anything about it?'

'Er, because you don't want to?' I answered.

'Because I'm with you,' he corrected, with an edge to his voice. 'So if I can do that for you, why can't you do the same for me?'

He could not have been more wrong, but getting into a massive debate right now would be a disaster, so I stroked his arm. 'Come on, you're getting wound up over nothing.'

'You would say that, wouldn't you?' he said, shrugging me off.

The band had entered another ballad phase and couples were drifting on to the floor, swaying and whispering sweet lovelies to each other in the way couples were supposed to.

'There's nothing dodgy going on.' I held on to his sleeve. 'Honestly.'

He smiled and nodded.

Phew. I breathed out, releasing the tension.

'Shall we get back to work now?' I asked tentatively.

'You can,' he said, standing up straight, 'but I've had enough. Get the Sugar Plum Fairy to help you.'

And he walked off.

By the time I'd picked my jaw up off the floor, he'd disappeared.

Doing the booth single-handed was frantic, but at least it swept thoughts of Toby to one side for a while. Luckily, the guests were super patient, but as I worked my way through the queue I was getting very stressed and very, very hot. And not in the sexy sense.

By the end of the evening I was sweating like a pig, definitely *not* feeling like a fox. My cheeks were aching from fake-smiling; my hair had frizzed up to audition for the role of badly permed sheep and, thanks to the moron who'd sloshed half a glass over me, I was reeking of red wine.

When I finally slumped against the empty booth I looked like a cross between an extra in a zombie movie and someone recently gored by a bull. And this was where Badger found me, my eyes half closed and prickling tears, clutching a life-size inflatable Elvis.

'Hi, Daisy,' he said, concern on his sweet face. 'Are you OK? Where's Toby?'

He left in a ridiculous paranoid mood over nothing was on the tip of my tongue, but I was too whacked to even go there.

'Had to get home,' I said finally, my throat a bag of splinters. I swallowed hard. *I will not cry, I will not cry.*

Gemma stepped forward, gently put her hand on my shoulder. 'Daisy, would you like some help?'

'That would be . . .' The tears were threatening to spill now. I cleared my throat. 'Yes, please. The props need to be packed up in those boxes.'

I unpopped Elvis's stopper and with a sad *pffft* he sagged in my arms, totally deflated. *You and me both, mate*, I thought.

From the glances and smiles as they worked, I could

tell Badger and Gemma were happy for the excuse to spend time together, which took some of the sting out of accepting help from one of the guests.

With everything back in the crates, we started loading the van alongside Dad.

He looked around. 'What happened to Toby?'

Good question. 'He had to go,' I said, shutting the lid on the costume hamper.

Then when we got back home, wonderful Dad said he'd unload the stuff, and I was so bone-knackered I didn't argue. Instead, I curled up in bed, falling immediately into a sleep coma and didn't come round till after ten the following morning.

I checked my phone the minute my eyelids creaked open, but there was no text, no voicemail, not one word from Toby the Lurch-leaver. I wasn't that surprised, but it didn't stop my heart sinking past my knees.

There was, however, a cheery message from Ayesha about the cinema date with all the boys. With everything that'd happened it had completely slipped my mind and the reminder sent my heart down through the floorboards: I'd have to explain Toby wouldn't be coming.

My hand was twitching, desperate to dial his number for a big shouty *I really liked you and you ruined it!* rant, but instead I wrapped it in an old jumper and threw it to the back of the wardrobe (the phone, that is, not my hand) to the sound of my self-esteem shouting, *For the love of God, do not waste another day of your life waiting to hear from a boy.*

After I'd banished my mobile I wandered downstairs and helped myself to a slice of leftover cake out of the tin. And another. And, because I'm a complete cakehead who doesn't give a toss, a third. I'd scoffed one of them down before I was even back in my room,

Cyberstalking: the mental equivalent of self-harming. I knew it would hurt, but I just couldn't help myself. Spying on Matt's antics via the Misery Machine (aka laptop) was a bad move when I was already eating my way into depression, but at least it was calorie-free.

Ouch. Every click was another cut. His Instagram feed resembled the 'after' pages of a spectacularly successful dating site. Golden, shimmery sunshine and laughter on gorgeous, happy faces. Matt and Rosa were smiling, they were laughing, they were having fun.

They were making me cry.

Desperate for distraction I went on another Google

manhunt, but there were just too many Toby Smiths, even when I added London as a filter. I stalked the guy until I was blue in the face – *zilch*. I stashed the laptop away at the back of the wardrobe beside my phone.

God, I was fed up.

The rest of the day involved box sets and books, anything I could, to put off revising for my maths test.

Ugh. I hated maths. I mean, I got why it was important, but I didn't get *it*. Any tiny glimmer of interest I might ever have had was obliterated by five years of regular humiliation on the razor edge of Mr Fox's tongue.

'Daisy Green, I say algebra and you stare at me with the vacant eyes of the recently lobotomised.'

Hilarious. No, really.

When I could avoid it no longer, I braced myself and made a start. But the more I tried, the more frustrated I got as the jumbled signs and numbers in front of me made their usual zero sense: *4 times what? 2b where? Who even needs to know this stuff?*

How stupid that your whole future could be decided on your ability to do something you wouldn't ever need to do again.

Maths GCSE, you can kiss my big, fat, number-phobic ass,

I thought, throwing the revision guide down in disgust. Matt + Toby = Misery Squared was the only equation that was making any sense to me today.

I flopped back on the bed and gazed at my bedroom ceiling. 'What am I going to do?' I moaned.

The ceiling stared back blankly. Useless, utterly useless. The door was more helpful though, creaking open to admit River. He padded in wearing his Yoda onesie and clutching Biohazard the Teddy in one hand, book in the other. 'Daisy, will you read me a story?' he said.

God, was it six thirty already? 'Course, little man.' I patted the bed. 'Hop on.'

'Love you, Daisy,' he said.

'Love you too,' I said, kissing the top of his curly mophead. Nice to know at least one member of the male species thought I was OK. By the time I'd reached the Big Fat Con (i.e. *and they all lived happily ever after*) he was half asleep so I led him back to his own bedroom.

And unless you count the continuing urge to kick Toby very hard in the babymakers, that snuggly interlude slightly cheered my mood.

I tried more maths avoidance by paying an overdue call on my To Be Read pile. But meh. After a few chapters, Perfect Book Boyfriend's mysterious moods and enigmatic silences had me dying to reach into the pages to slap his perfectly chiselled cheekbones.

Yes, I get you're troubled by a dark and secret angst. Yes, your soul is in greater torment than flesh and bone can bear. Yes, your aloof exterior masks a hidden vulnerability yada yada yada.

BUT JUST TALK TO HER.

Seriously, it'll save a load of hassle in the long run.

Fictional . . . real . . . whatever. Sick of romance and its rollercoaster twists and turns, I slammed the book shut with an *achhh!* of irritation and lay back on the bed, hands clasped behind my head. I had some heavy-duty brooding to do myself.

Didn't Toby claim to be some kind of maths whizz-kid? An IQ that put Stephen Hawking on a level with the average Big Brother housemate and he couldn't tell the difference between chatting *to* (as in *I am chatting to this man*) and chatting *up* (as in *is it hot in here or is it just you, baby?*)

How did that work?

Maybe it was because he hadn't known me long enough to realise I WOULDN'T CHEAT. Never had, never would. It just wasn't in my DNA.

So one minute I was feeling miserable and the next

I'd happily have had Toby dipped in honey and locked in a box of wasps. Or roasted on the breath of Satan's fieriest minion. Or forced to watch the home-shopping channel for eternity. And as I got into bed I was mainly thinking: *Why is he so stupid?*

Welcome to Paranoiaville.

Population: Toby.

CHAPTER 14

Woke up to find the laminated cover of *Hey, Let's Revise Maths!* stuck to my cheek.

Hey, Let's Not! I thought, unpeeling it with a painful *schwuck* before skimming it across the room.

I slumped back on the bed. What was the point of even getting up? Statistically speaking, the chances of me passing a test I'd barely revised for on a topic I didn't understand were . . . minus one per cent? One in none?

Don't ask me, I'm rubbish at statistics.

Even on a good day, a decent score would be borderline miraculous and I didn't need a crystal ball to tell me this wouldn't be one of those.

Hey, Let's Revise Maths! glared at me from the floor. Oh God, I was so failing this test. But I was determined not to spend today sobbing into my pillow. No, I would psych myself up for the moment I'd see Toby, maybe with his donkey mates in the canteen or with Flip-flop Phil in form. How should I react? Tell him he'd blown it when he abandoned me at the wedding? Absolutely.

You dropped me in it and now I'm dropping you. Attitude chosen, armour next. *Dress to make yourself happy* being my Rule *du jour*. Or *du life* actually.

Took me about five seconds to decide nothing says 'you're not even a blip on my emotional radar' than a pineapple-print sundress and pink Doc Martens. With a yellow cardie and bright pink lips, I looked *fierce*.

And as I arrived at college later, I was chanting the #1 Rule for Girls under my breath like a spell: *It's always better to be single, better to be single, better to be single . . .*

The double doors to the foyer slid open, sweeping me along with the tide of kids from the bus bays. Eight forty-five on the clock, plenty of time to get a coffee, find a lonely stairwell somewhere and make a last ditch attempt to revise. Maybe I could –

I stopped dead.

There was Toby, leaning against a pillar by the seating area, watching the entrance and looking so handsome and brooding I couldn't help but catch my breath.

If we were in a film, the screen would've gone wobbly round the edges. There'd be some time-lapse cinematography, visuals only because who needs dialogue when your souls broadcast on the same emotional frequency? The other students would blurrily speed past, leaving me and Toby suspended in our private moment, gazing meaningfully at each other while a romantic soundtrack swelled.

And my hair would look amazing.

But this was reality and reality didn't have a script, or at least not a decent one as far as my life was concerned. My hair was a ball of frizz and *I* might have stopped, but time carried on moving. As did everyone else coming through the doors behind me.

A lad with his eyes glued to his phone piled into me with such a smack, my bag flew to the floor. I staggered forward and he muttered, 'Watch where you're going, stupid cow.'

'Watch yourself, dumb-ass,' I snapped at his back.

Next thing I knew, a hand was steadying me and then my bag was back over my shoulder. Earlier I'd been idly pondering whether the contents of Toby's skull would wash off my boots, but hearing his voice say my name threw me, and in that hesitation he had his arm round my waist and was guiding me out of the crowd, towards an alcove at the side.

'I tried to ring you yesterday,' he said, standing close, using his back as a shield against the passing hordes.

'The battery was dead,' I lied, picturing my phone buried in the wardrobe.

He leaned further in. 'I wanted to explain about Saturday night.'

'I don't think there's anything you can say,' I said. More students were pouring in through the entrance and I spotted Gemma (wearing an amazing fox-print skirt) deep in conversation with . . . I craned my neck, yes! *Badger*.

'I deserve the chance to explain, don't I?'

Do you?

'You dropped me right in it. First you accused me of flirting with anything with a . . . a . . . man chromosome.' I ignored the amused expression that crossed his face. 'Which is something I completely never do. Then you were rude to a guest, which could've caused my mum and dad major problems. And then you buggered off, which is unbelievably crap. If I'd known you were going to flake out halfway through, I'd have asked one of my friends to help instead.'

A hot redness was creeping up my neck and I tugged my collar higher. 'So, frankly, I don't think there's anything left to explain because there's nothing you could say that would make any of that *not* have happened.'

And exhale.

'God, I am such an idiot sometimes.' He brushed his fringe out of his eyes in a way that would normally be bad-boy sexy, but today just bugged me.

I shrugged a *not disagreeing with you there, mate* and his eyes narrowed slightly. 'Look, I don't do grovelling,' he said, 'but I'd appreciate a chance to explain.'

'I haven't got time. I've got a maths test this afternoon.' *That I haven't revised for. Thanks to you.*

He clicked his fingers and pointed at me, thumb in the air, 'A maths test? Excellent.'

I hoicked my bag further up on my shoulder. 'Excellent for you maybe.'

'I mean, how about if I help you, then you listen to what I've got to say?'

Hmmmm.

Plan A (*Hey, Let's Revise Maths!*) had bombed and Plan B (temporary possession by the spirit of Einstein) had, frankly, always been a long shot.

Toby stepped closer and reached his hands up to

lean on the lintel of the alcove, exposing a good few centimetres of unbelievably toned brown stomach.

Hello, Plan C.

'Go on, let me,' he said, so quietly I had to tilt my head towards him. He smelled of clean clothes and mint. 'I want to make it up to you.'

He stroked my cheek and for a second I was almost hypnotised. Then I remembered the way I'd nearly cried at the wedding.

'If I pass,' I told him, stepping back, 'you get a chance to explain.'

He laughed and his hand fell. 'Of course you'll pass. I'm a numbers nerd, remember?'

'Well, I've got sociology now, but I'm free after that,' I said. 'I'll be —'

'I know where to find you,' he interrupted, reaching out to stroke my cheek again. 'See you in an hour then.'

He was already waiting in the corridor when I came out of the sociology classroom. I said bye to Badger, let Brittany's evil glare wash over me and walked across to where Numbers Nerd was leaning against the wall.

'You have no idea how allergic to maths I am,' I told him.

'I'll sort you out, I'm a mathematical wizard,' he answered with a smile.

'The Dumbledore of Decimals,' I said, half to myself.

'Dumble-what?'

'Beard? Harry Potter?' I said. 'You know.'

'Oh. Right. Not really.'

Somehow I managed not to die of shock as I followed him into the canteen. *Dumble-what?* It was like not knowing who God was.

He was frowning now as he thumbed through the pages of my textbook. 'Which bit are you struggling with?'

I winced. 'Um, all of it?'

According to Mr Fox, there were strains of plankton with greater mathematical ability than me. But having him as a teacher was what had made me maths-phobic in the first place.

Seated in a quietish corner, Toby took a pad of A4 and two pens out of his bag and pushed them in front of me. 'Equivalent fractions? You OK to start with that?'

Fractions. *Gulp*.

Panic teleported me back to Mr Fox's classroom. Tiny scribbled symbols covering every part of the board as he rambled on in . . . Parseltongue? Elvish? Not sure which. 'Sir, I don't get what you mean,' I'd said.

He had sighed theatrically. 'Your head is so empty that I'm amazed it doesn't just float away on the breeze. Stupid girl.'

No wonder my stomach gave an ominous *prepare to hurl* gurgle now.

'Don't stress,' Toby said, slapping the revision book on the desk. 'I promise I'll be gentle.'

And unbelievably, he was. Patient and clear, not mocking me when I messed up or he had to tell me the same obvious thing three times. Within five minutes, something was clicking. Ten minutes and the process made sense. Within fifteen, formerly dormant brain cells were lighting up like an epiphany machine until finally:

'I understand!'

He shot me an amused glance. 'Told you.'

'No, I mean I actually get it. Test me.'

He jotted some figures down on the pad and slid it across the table. 'There you go,' he said. 'See how you get on with those.'

Easy peasy.

Tick, tick, tick . . . as he marked my answers, Toby had that *Who's a clever little monkey?* look, the one Mum got when River put clean underpants on without being reminded.

Me? I was abso-freaking-lutely elated.

'In. Your. Face, Captain Comb-over,' I hissed, air-punching.

Eh? went Toby's expression, but I didn't care. Knowing I now had a chance in this test was great; knowing Mr Fox was wrong was *amazing*. I wanted to run up to St Mary's and fling the classroom door open. Shout, *I CAN do maths! I'm not a stupid girl, you're a rubbish teacher. And your hair fools no one.*

Then Toby leaned over and kissed me.

And I was so grateful, I let him.

CHAPTER 15

———

Yeeeeesss!

I bounded down the maths staircase like Tigger on Red Bull.

Woohoo!

Toby was sitting where I'd left him earlier, frowning over a game of Fruit Ninja. When I reached him, he gritted his teeth, squeezed one eye shut as if bracing himself for bad news. 'How'd you get on?'

'Smashed it! Totally.'

High five. 'Told you I was good, didn't I?' he grinned.

When I got out of bed this morning, it didn't even have a right side. But after acing this maths test, my world was suddenly shiny with all sorts of new possibilities.

'We should go and celebrate,' Toby yawned, stretching his arms above his head and slowly uncricking his neck. 'Do you fancy the Trafford Centre?'

Not as much as I fancy you, leched every cell in my body.

'Yeah, sounds good,' I answered.

Five minutes later, we were driving out of the college car park. A couple was standing at the zebra crossing and as Toby stopped to let them go, he said, 'Isn't that your mate Bodger?'

'Badger,' I said, spotting him. He was *holding hands* with Gemma!

I waved through the windscreen, but they only had eyes for each other. Gemma threw her head back and laughed at something Badger said and I smiled.

'What I wanted to say about Saturday night,' Toby said, 'is I might've got the wrong idea.'

Well, duh, I thought watching the happy couple disappear round the corner.

'Remember I said my dad went mental?' he continued.

'Yep,' I said. 'When he split up with your mum.'

He breathed out. 'Well, that's kind of why I lost it on Saturday.'

We'd stopped at traffic lights now. A magpie flew in front of the car, but I couldn't remember if one was for sorrow or joy. Toby put the handbrake on, turned to face me.

'Sometimes I get so mad I don't know what I'm saying or doing,' he said. 'I'm sorry you think I dropped you in it, but when I feel like that the best thing for me to do is get out of the situation till . . . till I calm down.'

'But there *wasn't* a "situation",' I pointed out. 'There was nothing for you to get mad about.'

'Dad should've got over the divorce ages ago, but he never has,' said Toby after a moment. 'I think it's kind of messed me up as well.'

The traffic light had turned to green and as we drove along he explained what happened with his parents. So far, so Jeremy Kyle: two couples who went on holiday together, had barbecues, did the pub quiz – all that couple-social stuff. Then Toby's mum started acting a bit shifty, going out with 'a friend', and his dad hit the roof.

'She had to get a restraining order in the end,' he continued, pulling into the car park. 'Because Dad came back one night and tried to smash the door down with an axe.'

'Oh my God,' I said.

'Yeah. It was like that bit in *The Shining*. You know, *Heeeeeere's Johnny.*' He snorted. 'Funny really. Mum had gone out. If he'd just rung the doorbell, I'd've let him in.'

He found a parking space and twisted to look behind as he reversed into it.

'How old were you?' I asked.

'Fifteen. The neighbours rang the police and they took him off in a riot van. I didn't see him again for weeks. That's when Mum and Jeff decided to move away.'

'That's awful,' I said, getting out.

The car bleeped as Toby locked the doors. When we got on the pavement he put his arm round my shoulders and carried on. 'I don't know what's worse. Being forced to live with Jeff or seeing my dad in that state.' A blast of warm air escaped from the entrance to the Trafford Centre as the automatic doors slid open.

'You OK with me getting a few things?' he said.

'Yeah, sure.' We stepped on the escalator together. 'So what's wrong with Jeff?'

'It'd be quicker to say what's *right* with Jeff.'

'Go on then. What's right about Jeff?'

'Nothing. He's a total headcase.'

Headcase. I had a sudden flashback to Ayesha's mum and Dan. 'He's not violent, is he?'

'Jeff?' Toby snorted loudly as we walked past the mannequins in the store entrance. 'Nah, he's just pathetic. I mean, he got my mum into power-walking.' He pulled a duck face, stuck his chest out. 'You know . . .' Elbows pumping and bum waggling, he stomped up and down looking so the opposite of King of Cool I couldn't help laughing. 'Jeff's a dick, but he's harmless. Honestly, it's like living with a Ned Flanders tribute act.'

I learned a lot about Jeff in the next couple of minutes. I found out he had a moustache that he trimmed with tiny scissors. He kept his change in a coin purse. Sometimes he wore cowboy boots. He smelled of Rich Tea biscuits.

'Oh yeah, and he snores so bad, Mum has to sleep in ear defenders. Even next door complained about the noise.'

'Does he make your mum happy?' I asked.

Toby paused, wrinkled his forehead. 'Yeah, I suppose so. Crazy.'

We wandered around for the next half an hour, going in and out of every hipster boy store in the centre, some so dark they really needed the price tags in Braille and a defibrillator on standby at the till. Toby was on a spending spree and I was trying to disguise the shock as he casually racked up bill after bill.

'Nothing like a good shop, is there?' he said. Words I immediately filed in the 'things I never thought I'd hear from a boy' department of my brain, along with the follow-up sentence: 'You've been dead patient. Let's get something for you.'

Being more of a vintage chick, I hardly ever shopped on the high street. And I'd never been in the store Toby was steering me towards now. This palace of hip, a store so exclusive even the shop-window dummies were sneering at my Mum-made outfit.

As we entered, I spied a velvet swing coat that had me drooling with garment-lust, but it wasn't designed for penniless urchins of my ilk.

'Toby, I couldn't afford a *coat hanger* in this place.'

'No one's asking you to,' he said. 'But I need to say sorry and you need a dress for that eighteenth party. Two birds, one stone.'

Did I hear him right? 'You want to buy me a dress? From here?'

'That's the plan,' he said, rifling through a rack. 'How about this one?' He plucked out a little black number.

Maybe some girls wouldn't be able to believe their luck. Maybe some girls would enjoy splurging someone else's cash. Maybe I am not some girls: truth is, I was kind of stunned.

'Do you want to try it on? This one's a . . .' he peered at the label, 'size 8.'

Size 8? I didn't know whether to feel flattered or depressed. The only size 8 parts of my body were my *feet*.

The price tag had my eyeballs nearly jumping out of their sockets. Mum did bespoke bridesmaid dresses for less with enough left over for colour-matched shoes.

'Toby, you can't buy me that. Have you seen how much it costs?'

His voice was low as he drew me close. 'Daisy, I need to do this to feel better about Saturday. Please let me.'

'Honestly, a latte and a choc-chip muffin would be more than enough,' I said. 'But considering you got me to pass a test on fractions, I think we're already quits.'

'Go on,' he said, 'at least try it on.'

I quickly checked the rail for my size. 'This one should fit,' I said, discreetly turning the label over as I held it up.

And yes, it was a beautiful dress. Well cut. Sophisticated. The material thick and expensive (to match the price tag). It was just very *different* from the kind of thing I usually wore. Plainer. Darker.

Still, I was excited as I swished it down over my shoulders in the changing room. I wiggled the skirt straight, half turned to check my rear view. Wished I'd worn the Belly Constrictors. Breathed in, tugged the zip up and went back out to the shop floor.

'Wow!' said Toby.

Wow indeed. The full-length mirror reflected a sleek and glamorous lady. Not a size 8 admittedly, but nipped in in the right places (even without anti-flab pants). Toby reached up and unfurled my hair from its messy, pen-skewered topknot. I'd definitely got the message he preferred my hair down.

'That's better,' he said as the girl in the mirror watched. She looked a couple of years older than me and chic. Stylish even. *Groomed*. Not words I could apply to myself very often. This was a girl who was really going places.

They just weren't the sort of places Daisy Green would go.

Toby took hold of my waist. 'That was quick. Most girls take hours.'

Most girls? I put that snippet away to dissect later and said, 'It's lovely, but not really my sort of thing. And it's way too expensive.'

'Don't be daft,' he said. 'If you look good, I look good so actually you're doing me a favour.'

He hugged me.

Then, over his shoulder, I spied a mannequin modelling a dress. This was no ordinary nice-but-safe Little Black Dress. *This* was a dress so far up my street, it had followed me home and started pounding on my wardrobe door.

I gazed at the parrot print, cute rounded collar and A-line skirt. An outfit jigsawed together in my mind that would be perfect for Tom's party: black opaques, Mum's velvet tuxedo jacket with the dragonfly brooch, red heels, ruby lipstick . . .

'What do you think of that one?' I said, gesturing at the dress-myself-happy dress of my dreams.

Toby took a quick, pained glance. '*Gross*. Forget the Grandma curtains and get changed,' he said. 'And I'll pay.'

Oh well.

Back in my natural habitat of quirky pineapple skirt, I joined him in the queue.

'Right. That's the dress for the party sorted, now we just need to get rid of those monsters,' he said, tapping my foot with the toe of his trainer.

Get rid of my beloved pink patent Docs?

'They're my favourite possessions in the whole

world,' I protested, laughing at the nonsense of the idea. 'If the house was on fire, I'd save these first. Well, after my family obviously. I *love* these boots.'

He raised his eyebrows. 'As did the gay builder you stole them off, I'm sure.' He was handing his debit card over. 'Next time, we'll get some proper shoes for you. You can't wear those with this.' He shook the carrier bag at me.

Maybe he was right; no way would the glammed-up girl in the mirror be seen dead in Doc Martens.

As Toby dropped me, my boots and the not-quite-me dress home, he said, 'I'll come back at six for the cinema, yeah?'

Lucky I hadn't sent that cancelling text to Ayesha after all. I nodded. 'And thank you for this. You really didn't need to,' I said. 'And for helping me with maths.'

He gave me a final kiss on the lips. 'No, thank *you* for forgiving me for Saturday and for letting me tell my side. I knew you'd understand.'

But it wasn't until I went to put my key in the lock that I realised, despite the stuff he'd told me about his parents splitting up over Freaky Jeff, I still didn't totally get 'his side'.

I'd learned way more than I needed about Jeff's personal grooming habits, but nothing about why Toby had gone ballistic over me talking to Badger and Rich the Best Man. Yes, his mum had had an affair and his dad had hang-ups, but what did that have to do with me?

And ugh! More to the point, what was that unholy stench?

'I think River's blocked the toilet again,' I shouted as I shut the front door behind me, relieved I hadn't invited Toby in.

'What's that, love?' Mum called out from the kitchen. 'I'm doing the dinner.'

'Nothing, doesn't matter,' I answered, going in. I peeked in the cauldron, sorry, *pan*, she was attending to on the hob. The contents looked (and smelled) as if they'd recently passed through a cow's digestive system.

My taste buds prepared to commit suicide. My mum was amazing at everything . . . except cooking, but no one had the heart to tell her.

'Where's Dad?' I asked.

'Taken River swimming. They should be back any minute,' she said, looking up. 'Oooh, have you been shopping? Is that a new dress?'

Mum had actual Spidey-sense when it came to clothes. Or X-ray vision. Whichever, she had an uncanny ability to pinpoint a clothing purchase even through the bag.

'Yeah.' I slid the dress out and held it against me. 'Check it out, Mum. It's for Tom's eighteenth.'

Her expert eye assessed it with one look. 'Beautifully made. Lovely fabric. And, far be it from me to tell you how to spend your money, extremely expensive.'

'Not my money, *Toby's*.'

'Really?' Surprised face.

'He said I could choose anything I liked, so I went for this.' Which was near enough to the truth.

'Right.' She stirred the green gloop, 'Well, it's gorgeous, but it's a big present from someone you've only just met.'

'He wanted to say sorry for rushing off on Saturday night.'

'Yeah, me and Dad were wondering what happened,' she said.

For a few seconds I was tempted to tell her about the paranoia stuff with the best man and Toby's issues with his parents' tangled love life. But I bit my lip.

'Something came up with his parents and he had to go.' (Technically, this wasn't a lie.)

She wrinkled her forehead. 'Well, it seems a bit extravagant. It's certainly a beautiful dress. Just . . .'

She paused and looked at me then back at the dress. Unusual this. Normally, she was a firm believer in the hands-off school of parenting.

'Just what?'

'Just . . . I know how much Matt meant to you, to all of us really. And I know how much his going away has upset you. I guess what I'm trying to say is, make sure you like Toby specifically because he's Toby, not because you're trying to replace Matt. Do you get what I mean?'

I nodded. 'Yeah.'

'Don't rush into anything. I know it's hard not to get carried away when you first start seeing someone.' She sighed, getting the dreamy oversharing eyes. 'When I think back to when me and your dad first –'

Wah! I pointed at the bubbling pan. 'Mum, don't let your beans are boil over.'

Distraction accomplished, I grabbed a handful of Dad's cherry cookies from the jar. 'No dinner for me, thanks, I'm eating out,' I shouted on my way up the stairs. I bit into a cookie as *hurray*! my taste buds lived to taste another day.

*

Ayesha's rationale for picking the cinema for our three-couple date was: 'You talk about the film before you go in. Sit for two hours. Come out and talk about what you've all seen. No tricky topics. No awkward silences. Simples.'

As a 'meet the boyfriends before the big eighteenth' plan, it was hard to fault. If I had one tiny niggle, it was how Toby might react to Shaney's neck tattoo and to minimise any chance of a public guffaw-athon/pant-wetting, I pre-warned him on the drive over.

When he'd finished snorting 'wonce', I had to extract a promise he wouldn't mention it. 'And please don't laugh either or Beth will literally never speak to me again.'

'Start praying he's wearing a polo neck,' Toby said.

Of course he wasn't (because he's not a cat burglar from the 1960s), but he'd turned his shirt collar up, so the tragic tatt was mainly hidden. We rendezvoused at the pick 'n' mix and I got my first good look at Beth's new boyfriend.

I'd seen the Instagram workout photos, so I was expecting tantastic, knobbly muscles, meaning the only shock was his utter nice-guy ordinariness. And Beth was simply glowing. Yes, total proof that one girl's frog really could be another girl's Prince Dreamy Trousers. She did the intros and Shaney leaned in to kiss me on the cheek, then held his hand out to Toby.

Eeek.

For a moment my brain played Worst-case Scenario, involving Shaney and Toby in Battle of the Alpha Males. Macho swaggering, chest-puffing, bone-crushing, Neanderthal knuckle-scraping – I waited for the cringe.

'Hiya, mate,' said Toby, shaking Shaney's hand.

And it was over. Phew. Relax. Then it was Tom 'sweetest man on earth's' turn and we'd sailed through the first possible flashpoint.

So it turned out Shaney was actually lovely. *Wonce* you got to know him. *Heh-heh.*

Popcorn pit stop over, the six of us strolled into Screen 10 together. As we took our seats everyone seemed great, but I was finding it mildly freaky being in the Toby-not-Matt dynamic.

The film was some action/stunt thing that Ayesha judged to have the least embarrassment potential. After the first couple of car chases, I started to relax and enjoy myself. Had a slight tense moment when Rugged Main Man started getting his frisk on with Impossibly Stunning Love Interest, but I stuffed popcorn in my mouth with incredible concentration until they'd finished.

We moved on to Stage 3: the pizza place without a hitch, where *Talk about what you've just seen* had evolved naturally into a game of *Wasn't she in that film with whatshisname who goes out with the skinny one from that TV thing?*

We were in the middle of debating this when the waiter appeared at my side. 'What can I get you?'

I swept my hungry eyes down the list of loaded skins, calzone, dough balls . . . Nah.

'Nachos with extra chilli, please.'

'It's free fries with a main on Mondays,' he said, pointing his pen at the special-offer sticker.

Nom nom. 'Go on then.'

Toby stared at me, wide-eyed. 'Nachos AND fries. Seriously? After all that popcorn?'

'Yep, I'm starving,' I said happily.

'*Okaaaay,*' he said, drawing the word out and slowly nodding while he looked at his own menu.

'What?' I said.

'Nothing. Nothing.' Then to the waiter. 'I'll have the chicken salad, thanks. I'm totally full after that *family bucket of popcorn.*'

I sighed, caught between irritation at the cheeky dig and a hint of *hmm, good point*.

'Actually, can I leave the fries?' I said to the waiter.

The food arrived and as we all tucked in, the conversation flowed easily from the film to Tom's eighteenth to Shaney's new job. Toby chipped in now and then with questions and laughs in the right places, and as I watched him at ease with my friends I caught myself taking another small step towards getting over Matt and forgetting about the weirdness at the wedding.

'Daisy, Beth.' Ayesha's words interrupted my thoughts. '*The Usual?*' She said in a deep and reverent voice.

'What's The Usual?' asked Toby, looking round the table.

Beth flipped through the menu to a full-page colour close-up. '*That* bad boy'

Megachoc Sundae. A tower of Rocky Road-esque chocolatey glory studded with fluffy marshmallows.

'Wow,' said Toby. 'That looks . . . calorific.'

My appetite screeched to a halt. 'Not this time,' I said, patting my belly like a supermarket Santa. 'I'll just have a coffee.' And I nudged away the plate of half-eaten nachos.

Beth gasped, clasping one hand in front of her mouth

in mock horror, 'Who are you and what have you done with Daisy Green?'

'Yeah, Daze, we always have the Megachoc Sundae,' said Ayesha. 'You ill or something, girl?'

'Just not hungry,' I said, pouring another glass of water.

'Serious?'

I shrugged and swirled the ice.

'Your loss, Gwyneth Paltrow,' she said, jabbing her fork into my leftovers. 'All the more for me and Beth.'

Toby squeezed my knee under the table and gave me a smile. I ordered a black coffee and focused on that as they ate, accompanying every mouthful with ecstatic groans of food love. It was torture.

It helped to visualise the new, expensive black dress currently hanging on my wardrobe door, waiting for an unflabby physique to wear it to a party.

I'd managed to dodge the food bullet and I was thinking the evening had gone amazingly well, when the conversation took a turn for the worse. While we were waiting for the bill, Ayesha and Beth started chatting about this new girl who'd started at school. It wasn't the first time they'd mentioned her and I'd seen her pop up online, but it was only now that I realised the true extent of their obsession.

'Jasmin's hilarious,' Ayesha was sniggering. 'So funny it's not true. You'd love this, Daze. She does this impression of Mr Fox . . .'

'Ha, yeah,' Beth gasped. 'She's got your old desk, you know, by the window. And she opened it and called him over and . . .'

'It was dead windy,' said Ayesha. 'So when he turned round, the draught got under it and . . .'

Beth mimed a comb-over flipping up like a toilet lid. 'The whole thing lifted – ha ha – in – in – one piece . . .'

Ayesha continued, twitching of limb and scarlet of face. 'And he was so mad that . . . that . . .'

But Mr Fox's reaction was lost to uncontrollable giggles. The girls clutched each other's shoulders while we stared at them. The boys in amusement, me not so much.

Maybe you had to be there, eh?

'Someone's got a major girl crush,' said Beth, blowing her nose on a serviette.

'So have you!' Ayesha protested. 'God, Daze, you wouldn't believe the stunt she pulled in form time.'

'Yeah!' exclaimed Beth, slapping the table. 'God . . . God . . . God . . . when she put that toi . . . toilet br–'

'*Toilet brush!*' squawked Ayesha in between yelps.

But the Amazing Jasmin's jolly jape disappeared into wordless screeching, so I never did find out what crazy prank she pulled.

Shame that.

They were still in hysterics as we walked into the car park. 'She sounds simply incredible,' I said. But she didn't; she just sounded simple. I mean, a toilet brush?

'Form is completely different now,' said Beth. 'It's *such* a laugh.'

Ayesha unintentionally twisted the knife in further. 'You know we were worried how the footie team would do without you? Jasmin has been brilliant. She's taken your place completely.'

My friends, my desk, my team, my position on Mr Fox's Most Hated list. The Amazing Jasmin had apparently got the lot.

She's taken your place completely.

I half wondered if I'd get home later and find my parents had packed my bags and adopted her.

My eyes started prickling and I swallowed hard as I reached for a tissue, mumbling, 'Must be getting a cold.' But they were too wrapped up in rampant fangirling to notice me anyway.

Toby did though. He wrapped both arms round me

and pulled me in close. I put my chin up and blinked quickly.

'So, it's Jasmin's birthday on Friday,' Beth was saying.

Well, whoop-dee-doo. I thought.

'We're going uptown,' Ayesha told me. 'She's dying to meet you, Daze.'

'Are boyfriends invited?' said Toby.

My *What, let her try to steal you too?* thought was followed swiftly by, *Did you just refer to yourself as my boyfriend?!*

'Girls' nights out are strictly no boys allowed,' Ayesha told him before I had a chance to open my mouth. 'Mates before men. It's a Girl Rule set in stone.' Ayesha turned her head. 'Sorry, Shaney, that means you too.'

He shrugged and held his hands palm outwards in a *that's fine* gesture. 'Trust me, no need to apologise. I saw enough girls' nights out at The Rat and Drainpipe to last me a lifetime.'

'Yep, count me out too,' added Tom.

'We're doing the early bird at Balti Towers,' Ayesha continued. 'Then uptown for a spot of general mischief. Sound OK?'

'Yeah, good,' I managed.

'And what time do you expect this orgy of girly mayhem to end?' asked Toby.

'Girly mayhem will go on till well after midnight.' Ayesha looked at me quizzically, and danced a little jig on the spot. 'Daze, game on?'

'We're doing a wedding on Saturday,' I said, in a flat voice. 'It might be a bit late if I've got to work all day. Let me think about it.'

'Oh,' said Ayesha. She buttoned her coat. 'Right. Well, let me know so I can tell her how many seats to book in the restaurant. We could always order you an earlier cab.'

'Come on, Daze!' said Beth, with a jokey punch on my arm. 'It'll be great. You're going to love Jasmin.'

I smiled tightly, repeated. 'I'll need to think about it.'

Then we were saying our goodbyes and everything was fine. On the surface at least.

'Are you OK?' asked Toby as we drove home. 'You've gone very quiet.'

'Just a bit tired,' I said. 'Did you have a good night?'

'Yeah, the film wasn't the best, but I like your friends.'

That was good news at least.

He laughed. 'They can't half put some food away. I don't understand how they're both so skinny.'

'I know, lucky girls,' I said. My stomach was building up to a massive indignant rumble of deprivation. *Unfinished nachos? No pudding?* I was starving.

We'd parked up near the house now and there was a real danger that if he went in for the kiss, I'd end up gnawing his head off.

He cupped his hands round my face. 'Well, I'm sure they wish they were as beautiful as you.'

I managed a semi-smile before he dived in for some steamy, snog-based action. But the whole time my head was going, *Are you calling me fat?* Because that's basically what he was getting at, wasn't it?

I was having weird thoughts as I got ready for bed. The alpha-male antler-locking I'd been stressing about never happened, but things I hadn't seen coming were making me miserable. I didn't want Toby thinking I was beautiful *despite* my size. I just wanted him to think I was beautiful.

I was on the edge of sleep when the phone beeped with a message from Ayesha. *I didn't want to say anything with Toby there, but Matt's coming over for the party. Thought you'd want to know xxxxx*

Instantly awake, my hand shook as I swiped to open the Facebook app. I swear I didn't want to, but my fingers were things possessed, typing Matt's name in as my helpless brain looked on.

Under his latest status of *Coming home!* there were

211

loads of comments, all variations on *Looking forward to seeing you, mate.*

Scroll, scroll, scroll. Stop. One comment from Ayesha leaped off the screen.

Can't wait to meet Rosa! xx

If I was a cartoon character my eyes would have boinged out on springs. I realise Ayesha and Tom have been friends with Matt since Year 7 too, but still . . . *ouch.*

To top it off, Facebook pinged.

Jasmin Newton has sent you a friend request. Confirm or ignore?

I pressed *ignore.*

CHAPTER 16

How do you know you're officially an item?

First kiss? When a guy calls himself your boyfriend in front of all your mates? When you hug your phone when you get a midnight message that says **Missing you? xx**

Without having the *where are we at then?* convo it was hard to be certain. But for the rest of the week my seat was saved in the canteen along with a very public kiss when I got there. We'd been for after-college drinks, had another shopping expedition and he'd turned up again at footie training to take me and Ayesha home.

So by the time Friday lunchtime rolled around, all the signs pointed to us being a genuine item, even if neither of us had said the words.

I'd got to the canteen a few minutes early. Mozz

and Jozz, etc. were herding in Donkey Corner, loudly competing for the position of Biggest Idiot (a close-fought battle). But no Toby.

I scanned the canteen for Badger or Gemma, but there was no sign of them either. Bench after bench was crowded with groups of people I didn't know, eating or playing cards. Even where there was the odd space I could hardly walk up and squeeze myself in, could I? A big arrow with No Mates! followed me round the canteen as I desperately tried to think of how to wait inconspicuously.

Behold, fellow students, as Daisy Green nonchalantly approaches the Information Zone. She just loves chillin' with the leaflets. Mind like a sponge soaking up all that information. Dealing with Exam Stress. Top Ten Healthy Eating Tips. Stub Out Smoking Today . . .

What's that? She's reading leaflets to disguise the fact she has no friends? Rubbish! Allergic Rhinitis and You *is essential reading for any modern teen.*

I was rescued by a familiar waft of lemony-cottony-mintiness, followed by a kiss next to my ear. The hairs on my neck stood on end and I shivered. (In a good way.)

'Hello, gorgeous,' said Toby. 'What you up to?'

'Oh, hi,' I said casually. 'Nothing much, you know. Catching up on some stuff.'

Picking up a random leaflet, I flapped it around as a convincing prop. Toby caught my wrist mid-wave, tilted his head and angled the leaflet towards him.

'Help! I've got chlamydia,' he read loudly. 'What are my treatment opt—'

All hail the Queen of Twatania.

I tugged the leaflet out of his grasp and frantically stuffed it back in the rack. Well-versed as I was in the art of auto-humiliation, this was excruciating.

'Shall we go and sit down?' he said with a smirk.

At least Brittany's wet-look leggings cheered me up with a farty squeak as she slid along the bench to let Toby in. I caught the inside of my cheek in my teeth and tried (unsuccessfully) not to snigger.

'Hi, Toby,' she said, giving him a flirty once-over. 'Hi, Debbie,' she said, giving me the evil eye.

'Daisy,' corrected Toby.

'Why do I always get it wrong?' she said with a fake smile.

I fake-smiled back. *Because you're a cow?*

There was some hard-core, hereditary evil at play here. No one could possibly *learn* that level of bitchcraft;

it's something she had to be born with, like six fingers or a tail. But Rule #9 told me I must *Rise above bitchiness.* Sitting so close to Brittany, this was obviously difficult, but I tried.

The donkeys were chatting about some charity five-a-side against the teachers they'd signed up for.

'Daisy's on a football team,' said Toby in a tone that made me look twice. Was he making fun of me?

'Used to be on two,' I corrected. 'My old school and Town Ladies. But I can't do matches because of work so I just train twice a week nowadays. And college hasn't got a team.'

'*Ladies*' football?' scoffed Jozz (predictably).

'Nothing ladylike about girls' football,' said Toby with a laugh. 'I've seen them in action – it's total carnage.'

'How about you, Brittany?' said Jozz with a leer. 'Would you fancy getting all down and dirty with a bunch of girls?'

She shuddered. '*Eeew*. Me? Play soccer? Look at me.' She gestured at her own body, skinny as a model's, and did a bit of a wiggle. 'You have to be kind of husky to play those man sports,' she continued, with a wave in my direction. 'No offence, Debbie.'

HUSKY?

'That's the classic misconception about women's football,' I said. 'Fitness is the most important quality in a player meaning even the scrawniest girls can play.' I paused before adding, 'No offence.'

Touché.

She shot me a filthy look then batted her eyelashes at Jozz. 'I think I'll stick to cheerleading, honey. I'm useless around balls.'

'Ahem,' comedy-coughed her charmless boyfriend with a suggestive grin. Brittany giggled and joke-slapped Jozz, mock outrage on her face. Then suddenly the two of them were snogging right next to us with actual audible slurps. Ugh.

One of the others (Mozz? Bozz? Tozz?) regarded me, a puzzled expression spreading over his donkey-like features.

'Aren't girl footballers all lezzers?'

I pictured banging my head on the table.

'Some are gay, yes. But the players' sexuality isn't really relevant, is it?' I rolled my eyes. 'What century do you live in?'

He leaned back, palms spread. 'Easy, love. I'm just saying.' He looked at Toby, 'Mate, you've got a live wire here.'

I pictured banging *his* head on the table. Blood, gore, bone. Peanut for a brain.

'Don't be so sexist, Mozz,' Toby said. 'Women's football is a growing sport.'

Thank you! Encouraged, I agreed. 'It is. The Women's World Cup gets loads of coverage and even we've had quite big crowds at some matches.'

Jozz and Brittany had surfaced from their snog, like a pair of dolphins coming up for air. Only not intelligent or cute.

Jozz adjusted his crotch. My eyes retched.

'Girls' football's something new. Exciting.' *Yes! Go Toby.* 'Think about it: with men, you expect a high level of precision and skill, but with girls, who knows?'

Erm . . .

'Yeah, s'pose,' Mozz nodded. 'Interesting in a car-crash way. Like who's going to fall over next. Or score an own goal. Or cry. I get that.'

I heard a snigger from Brittany's direction.

'Not quite,' I said. 'In fact –'

I gave up. Bozz (?) had arrived with doughnuts and no one was listening.

'I'd better go,' I said to Toby.

'OK. Walk you to Spanish?'

'Sure,' I said, sliding along the bench.

'Take no notice of Mozz,' Toby said when we were halfway down the corridor. 'He doesn't know what he's talking about.'

'I was the captain of the team at school, you know,' I told him. 'And Town Ladies won the County Cup last year.'

'I'm not saying you're no good,' he said. 'Just that it's an unusual hobby for a girl, especially one like you. You know, a pretty one. Most girls do cheerleading or horse riding or skiing. Stuff like that.'

I stopped and turned to face him. 'It's called football cos you play it with your feet. Look —' I waved one Doc Marten-clad leg in the air. 'Wow, girls have feet too.'

He winced down at my boots. 'We have got to get you some proper girl shoes.'

'I've got loads of proper girl shoes,' I said stubbornly. 'I just love these best.'

'No wonder Mozz thinks you're gay.' He shook his head.

Five hours later, and after a particularly gruelling training session, I'd swapped my football boots for 'proper' girly footwear in honour of the Amazing Jasmin's Balti Towers birthday bash.

Yay, supreme.

And as if dripping with sweat after power-hobbling from the bus station wasn't sufficiently awesome, the air con in the restaurant was bust. On top of that, my dress appeared to have shrunk since its previous outing for Beth's birthday in April.

Obviously it was washing machine's fault that the cap sleeves were digging into my arms; that the skirt was so narrow my knees fused together into one big knee, forcing me to hobble in tiny hoppy steps; that the seams creaked ominously with every breath. And as if all that wasn't enough, I had the beginnings of an almighty headache niggling.

I arrived at the restaurant in the worst possible mood and I hadn't even met the Amazing Jasmin yet. As I wove through the tables, I was thinking, *Come on, give me an excuse to hate you. Be irritating or sulky or stinky or —*

'Daisy!' she shouted, sending the balloons bobbing around her chair as she jumped up. 'I'm so glad you could make it!' She folded me into a hug. 'I've been dying to meet you!'

'Um, thanks. Happy birthday.' I hugged her back noticing one of us did indeed smell bad — and it wasn't Jasmin.

'Thank you! Come and sit down,' she sing-songed, dragging out a chair. I waved hello round the table at the St Mary's gang and within minutes I was following a selection of different conversational threads. I tuned in on one which sounded familiar: Beth moaning about a man.

'Teething troubles,' Ayesha was saying. 'Perfectly normal part of a new relationship.'

'But he's so *tidy*!' moaned Beth. 'Every time I go round, if I don't wash up a tea mug within like one second of finishing he does this.'

She demonstrated a very mild frown.

'It'll be OK,' I said. 'That's why they're called teething troubles: you grow out of them.'

'And he has this fear of running out of stuff so he hoards,' she went on. 'Toilet rolls, washing up liquid, whatever. He's got Cillit Bang coming out of his ears.'

'Sounds painful,' I muttered.

'Well, Tom's been laid-back since day one and it bugs me now more than ever,' said Ayesha with a grimace. 'Like, the arrangements for the party. He thinks buffets just spontaneously happen. Me and his mum ask him about the venue, the menu, the music. Nothing.' She waved her hand in front of blank eyes. 'It's like arranging

a party for a coma victim. Anyway, what about Toby?'
She turned my way, raising her voice over the noisy lads
behind us. 'Please tell me Mr Perfect has got some faults.
Does he not listen? Eat with his mouth open?'

'Is he soap-phobic?' added Beth with a shudder, the
memory of Stinky Pete still strong.

'Erm, no gross habits that I've noticed,' I said,
dunking my poppadum in the mango chutney. 'Decent
table manners; on friendly terms with the shower. Good,
no, *very* good listener – pretty perfect all round in fact.'

'No one's perfect,' insisted Ayesha, before smugly
adding, 'except us of course. Come on, there must be
something. Make us feel better.'

'Or we'll get all jealous,' said Beth, 'and cry.'

'Um, I suppose he gets a bit jealous,' I said. 'You
know, paranoid if I talk to other men. Or about them.'

Putting one foot in my mouth while kicking myself
with the other was textbook me behaviour. I should have
realised the P-word was guaranteed to send Ayesha's
imagination spiralling down every possible wrong turn.

'What do you mean by "paranoid"?' she said.

'I didn't mean paranoid exactly,' I said with a hasty
backtrack. 'More, um, concerned.'

I really wanted her take on how Toby read the

wedding situation wrong and how he'd (kind of) explained why afterwards so I (kind of) got his point. But Ayesha viewed things from a suspicious perspective since Psycho Dan. Whatever the opposite of rose-tinted glasses were, Ayesha wore them and I knew she'd freak. I was so not up for public freakage.

'Fancy another poppadum?' said Beth lifting up the plate.

'Better not,' I answered. 'So what other annoying habits has Shaney got then? Not that I think tidiness is a negative. In fact –'

'Daisy,' Ayesha cut me off, 'what do you mean by paranoid?'

Sludge-tinted glasses, that was it. The ability to cast a gloomy glow over every sentence.

I sighed. 'Not paranoid, that's the wrong word. Just a couple of misunderstandings. No biggie.'

Before she could launch into a totally unnecessary lecture on Warning Signs, Jasmin plonked herself between us. Phew.

'You know, I came this close' – she pinched her finger and thumb together – 'to going to your college.'

'Oh, really?' I answered, swigging back some water. God, it was hotter than the sun in the restaurant.

'How come you ended up at St Mary's then?'

Ayesha was still watching me with a slight frown. I shifted in my seat, just enough to avoid catching her eye.

'My mum and dad.' Jasmin said. 'And the journey. School's walking distance from our new house. Worth the bus ride though. I thought the open day was great.'

'Don't you like St Mary's?'

'Like it? I *love* it.' She grinned wickedly, gestured round the table. 'These girls are just the best, aren't they?'

I looked at everyone laughing and chatting. 'Yes they are,' I said sadly.

And to my immense disappointment, the Amazing Jasmin was turning out to be as entertaining and funny as the rest of my friends. I tried my best to hate her, but it was literally impossible. She was lovely.

The evening should've been no different from old times, gossiping about school and boys and stuff. But it was. Not completely, I mean I wasn't visiting Planet Donkeybrain like with Toby's friends. But something had nudged me one step outside the circle.

The chat moved on to Tom's eighteenth birthday party, which was working up to becoming the biggest social event of the year. And that's when I twigged.

No one was mentioning Matt going.

Maybe they'd agreed it before I got there. *Don't talk about Matt. Especially don't say a word about his new girlfriend.*

And I knew it was to protect me, and I knew I had plenty to brag about in Toby, but it just made me unbelievably sad. As if me and Matt had never actually happened.

My phone vibrated on the table and I tapped the text open.

Send me a pic so I can see how gorgeous you look, T xxx

In the middle of mourning my old life, Toby was reminding me I had a new reason to smile. He really was perfect.

I quickly touched up my powder and lip-gloss, smoothed my hair down. Then sucking in my cheekbones, I pulled my finest selfie pout. *Click* and off it went, just as the food arrived.

'What you doing?' asked Ayesha.

'Toby wanted to see how gorgeous I look.' I grinned then put my phone down and didn't give it another thought.

My curry was delish, but it would have left a

professional fire-eater gasping for air. Not that there was any of *that* in Balti Towers: the seats were so close we were nearly sitting on each other's knees.

Behind us, the gang of lads was getting louder and there was mucho banter flying between our two tables, meaning every time I did try to chat I had to shout to be heard.

My head was throbbing, and my dress squeezed and creaked until I was petrified the seams would pop. But the worst of it was, surrounded by the people I knew best in the world, I felt *lonely*.

By the time we'd left the restaurant and walked into a bar, every squeal and giggle was going right through me. I was longing to lie down in my bed, pull the cool covers over my head and sleep. So when Toby texted at half eleven to say he was in town and did I want a lift home I almost sobbed with gratitude.

'Ayesha.' I grabbed her arm. 'I'm going to call it a night. I can't face a club.'

Next to her, Jasmin was looking at me in concern. 'Are you OK?'

'My head's banging. Sorry,' I answered. 'Thanks for inviting me though.'

'Poor you,' said Ayesha, bending to scoop her

handbag off the floor. 'Come on, I'll walk you to the taxi rank.'

I put a hand on her shoulder. 'It's OK, Toby's coming to pick me up.'

'*Aw*. That's so sweet!' Beth and Jasmin made *bless him* faces.

Ayesha kept hold of her bag. 'Are you absolutely sure?'

My phone pinged in reply: Toby was outside. I waved a general goodbye and promised Ayesha I'd text as soon as I got home.

Within seconds, I'd left the noise and heat and stepped out into the cool air. *Bliss.* I paused by the door, eyes closed for a second to let a wave of pain settle.

Toby was watching from across the road, elbow propped on the open window as I hop-hobbled to the idling car.

'God, *thank* you for picking me up. You're a mind-reader,' I said as I got in. 'My skull is about to explode.'

I leaned over to kiss him on the cheek.

'Have a good time then, did you?' he said.

'Not really,' I answered. 'I've had a headache all night.'

I got a sinking feeling in the pit of my stomach that had nothing to do with the fiery bhuna and everything to do with Toby's chilly tone. *Oh, not now*, *Toby,* I thought and tugged the hem of the too-tight skirt as far towards my knees as it would go. Even sitting down, my swollen toes were sawn in half by the stupid sandals.

I found the button and opened the window a few centimetres.

'Can you not do that, please,' Toby said, clipping each word. 'It's freezing.'

My head was still throbbing, but I closed it anyway, too tired to argue, and soon we were heading down the dual carriageway in uncomfortable silence.

I cracked first. 'Did you have a nice evening?'

'Not really,' he said.

We carried on driving: me, him and his weird-ass mood. I pressed my forehead against the glass and shut my eyes, thinking of home where my lovely soft pillow waited. *Won't be long now, won't be long now* went the wheels.

The click of the indicator came too soon. The rhythm of the car changed from smooth tarmac and my forehead bumped against the window. There was a crunch of gravel under the tyres as we slowed down.

'Where are we?' I asked, confused.

Killing the headlights, Toby put the handbrake on, plucked his phone out of his pocket and held it in front of me.

'What's this about then?'

The sudden illumination made me wince. As I focused on the screen, his silence, his mood, his picking me up all slotted into place. 'This' was my selfie from the restaurant. The first thing I noticed were my boobs spilling out under my flustered face. A sweaty pink mess. Embarrassing. But there was something else too, something I hadn't noticed at the time. Or rather some*one*. A total stranger was standing behind my chair, with a leery grin on his beery face and hands pressed together like he was about to dive down my cleavage.

Oh.

I could've kicked myself. *Why didn't I check it before I pressed send?*

'Who is he?' demanded Toby.

'I have absolutely no idea,' I said slowly. 'Honestly, I didn't even know he was there.'

My eyes were adjusting to the gloom and I realised we were in some kind of lay-by surrounded on three sides by trees. It was very very dark.

Toby's voice wasn't angry or cold, just disappointed. 'I thought I could trust you.'

'You *can*,' I said, slumping back in the seat. 'I told you, I've never seen him before in my life. Look, can we talk about it tomorrow? Please. I really need to lie down.'

He shook the phone at me, 'You sent this at eight forty-two and it's' – he checked the dashboard – 'eleven forty-eight. That's over three hours ago. How do I know you weren't with him the whole evening?'

The blood was pounding in my temples so hard I'd've cheerfully sold my soul for a big glass of water and a paracetamol. 'Because I'm telling you I wasn't. Come on. Tell me what you did tonight. Were you out with the lads?'

'Stop trying to change the subject,' said Toby, louder now. 'Don't you have any respect for me? For *yourself*?'

I rubbed my eye sockets with the heels of my hands; anything to ease the blinding tension. 'It's not my fault if some random sleaze-weasel photobombs me.'

'Look at what you're wearing!' he said. 'Of *course* it's your fault!'

If I hadn't been in agony, I'd've laughed. It was like I was out with Beth's dad. I propped my elbows on my knees and, eyes closed, rested my forehead on my hands. I couldn't deal with this now.

'*Please* will you take me home?'

He humphed. 'So I'm your taxi driver now, am I.'

I was in too much pain to argue that *he'd* called *me* and my patience had all but evaporated. 'Look at the photo, Toby. The guy's *behind* me, it couldn't be more obvious that I didn't know he was there. You're being ridiculous.'

Instead of starting up the engine, Toby leaned across me and I heard the door handle click.

'What are you doing?' I asked, peeping through splayed fingers.

'Get out of my car.' He pushed the door open.

'What?' I said stupidly. '*Here?* How am I supposed to get home?'

He turned the key and started revving the engine. 'You should've thought of that before.'

'Before what?' I said, dazed.

'Before you took me for a mug.'

So because I didn't know what else to do, I unbuckled my seat belt and lifted my bag out of the footwell. And I don't think my mind caught up with what was happening until the mini's tail lights had disappeared up the road and a cold gust of wind woke me up like a slap.

Toby had just dumped me in a lay-by in the middle of nowhere.

The part of me that wasn't in agony felt like

running after the car, yelling at Toby to come back. Instead I shivered, gazing around the darkness, kind of recognising where I was and knowing it was a long way from home.

Something rustled in the shadows and I literally jumped, panic shooting pain spikes through my skull. I felt sick now. The stinging cold and the dark pressed in on me as I rifled for my phone and, using the screen as a torch, I bent down to unfasten the stupid sandals. Gravel bit into the soles of my feet, but the relief of taking the vicious toe stranglers off made up for it.

Miles from anywhere, lost, confused and wearing a dress that barely covered my bum? This was a trailer for a bad horror movie, where every passing car was driven by a serial killer, every noise from the trees a murderer-to-be. I was almost in tears picturing my cosy pyjamas and warm bed waiting at home.

Walking was out and I was too shaken up to sit in a cab on my own, even if I'd had enough money left to pay the fare from here. Scrolling down my contacts list, my finger hovered over Dad Mobile. It was so late, I'd wake the whole house up and we had such an early start tomorrow. I rang Ayesha. If she didn't answer, I'd have to ring Dad.

Then it started to rain.

Oh joy.

It wasn't even twenty minutes later, but by the time Ayesha arrived, my teeth were chattering from the wet, the cold or the fear. Possibly a combination of all three.

'God, look at you!' she exclaimed, pointing at the dirty tatters where my feet used to be. 'What the hell?' She took her cardie off and wrapped it round me as I climbed in the taxi.

I was putting an answer together when I saw a black mini slow down on the opposite side of the road. I didn't need to see the driver to know who it was.

I saw my face reflected in the taxi window as we drove away. Hair plastered down, racoon mascara around the eyes of a pale, frightened girl.

'What happened?' said Ayesha gently. 'I thought Toby was giving you a lift.'

'I can't talk about it now,' I said. 'I'm in agony.'

She nodded. 'OK, just one thing. How did you end up in the middle of nowhere?'

'I don't know,' I said. I shut my eyes and when I opened them she was still watching me with a worried frown.

'Did you have an argument?'

'Yes, but I don't want to talk about it.' She sucked in her breath and let it out slowly. For the rest of the ride I leaned my head on her shoulder and kept my eyes closed.

It wasn't until we pulled up outside my house that either of us spoke again.

'I'm sorry for wrecking your night,' I said. 'I know you were having a good time.'

'Daisy, don't be daft,' Ayesha said. 'Do you want me to come in with you?'

'No, I'll be fine,' I said.

'I'll ring tomorrow, OK?' She had concern written across her face. I went to open the door, but she put a restraining hand on my arm. 'You have to promise me that if Toby left you in that lay-by on purpose, you'll never speak to him again.'

'Promise.' I hitched my bag on to my shoulder.

'No answering the phone or reading texts?' she insisted.

'I swear I will never speak to Toby Smith again,' I said.

'This is serious,' she said, hugging me. 'Him leaving you there, it's very bad. You understand?'

And then I was indoors at last.

As soon as I got to my room, I took two paracetamols, peeled the too-tight wet dress off and crawled into bed. I had thought I'd start crying, but I just wrapped myself tightly in the duvet and my last thought before I fell asleep was, *I am NEVER speaking to Toby Smith again.*

CHAPTER 17

I woke up to River's hand round my ankle, attempting to drag me out of bed.

'Daisy, Mummy says you have to get up now.'

Another Saturday. Another wedding.

I groaned and rolled over, but I knew I couldn't go back to sleep. There was a day of celebrating two people in love to get through first. Celebrate love? Ha. I'd rather eat broken glass.

And it appeared I already had. Well, walked on it anyway. I inspected the sole of each foot. They were covered in little cuts and scratches and huge bubble-wrap blisters where the vicious sandal straps had rubbed. Ouch.

'Come *on*,' said River, still trying to drag me off the bed. 'Mum *says*.'

Somehow I summoned up enough willpower to autopilot myself through a shower and into a dress and make-up and out of the house.

'You're quiet this morning,' said Dad as we loaded the gear.

'Bit of a headache,' I answered. 'I'll be fine.'

By the time we got to the ring road, I'd taken all the things I'd hoped might happen with Toby and buried them as deeply as I could. Then I drew a line under him. Not just any old line either. A barbed-wire barricade with armed guards ready to shoot down any stray, Toby-shaped thoughts that dared to sneak across.

The worst of the headache had faded with sleep and painkillers. Dad had the windows open and the breeze eased away the last dull throb so, by the time we reached the venue, my sore feet were the only physical reminder of last night's awfulness.

Ayesha had texted first thing to check how I was and also to remind me to 'cut that scumbag dead'. As if I'd do anything else.

Mum was at the bride's house and would be along later. Something Blue weren't playing; the couple had hired a DJ for the whole evening, which made me feel some guilty relief. Badger's brand of cheery loveliness would surely have tipped me over the edge today.

We'd never done an event here before, a sprawling Victorian hall in the middle of the roughest part of town, and I wasn't keen on how it looked from the outside. There was a scruffy transit van already there with a scruffy man I kind of recognised in the driver's seat, furiously yelling into a mobile and smoking.

My heart sank.

'Dad, tell me that's not Quality Catering.'

''Fraid so,' he said with a grimace.

Mum and Dad had a long list of good foodie companies they usually recommended to the bride and groom, but it looked like this time no one had asked to see it. We'd worked with every catering company for fifty miles over the years and all of them had been fantastic, with a single notable exception.

There was a special circle of gastronomic hell reserved for Quality Catering. We'd only done one wedding with them before, but it was highly memorable for all the wrong reasons. Oh yes, that pork pie may have shot through my digestive system like greased lightning, but the memory lingered.

'They've had their hygiene certificate reinstated,' Dad went on, 'but your mum's bringing sandwiches for us, just in case.' There was a pause, then he added, 'And extra loo roll.'

Dad went off with the caretaker to unpadlock the security shutters and take the grille off the main entrance while I unloaded the first boxes off the van. I heard loud beeps as they deactivated the security system and the slamming back of the bolts to the main reception room. Mr Ironically Named Catering stubbed his fag out and went in after them, arms full of foil-covered trays.

'What's the theme for the do again?' I asked, handing Dad a box of camera equipment when he reappeared.

'Hollywood Glamour.' He gave a friendly wave to a bunch of feral kids wheelie-ing round the van and the one at the front flipped him the finger.

'Stay with the van while I take this in,' he said in an undertone.

We didn't go to the ceremony with Mum, but she told us the groom, Mark, decided to liven things up with his unique brand of comedy. (And by unique she meant desperately unfunny.) By the time the happy couple reached the hall, you could've cut the atmosphere with a knife.

In fact, substitute 'atmosphere' for 'groom' and that was the bride's parents. They were dressed head to foot in black and stony-faced as a couple of graveside statues, mother in a fascinator recycled from avian roadkill, father staring murderously into the middle distance.

Yep, the photos weren't the best.

And neither were the speeches. Since Something Borrowed had started, I'd heard funny speeches; touching speeches; tearful ones; ones so boring, I nodded off. But never anything quite like these.

His expression may have been murderous, but the bride's dad was a slight man, stooped, with all the gravitas of a world-weary gerbil as he took a crumpled sheet of paper from his jacket pocket.

'Monica has always been a stubborn girl,' he began in a voice as trembly as his hands. 'From the moment she was born, she never listened to a word of advice from me or her mother.'

There were some hesitant tittering laughs.

'When she turned eighteen and we asked her what use was a marketing degree, she ignored us. Credit cards, car loans, unwise flat-sharing – Marjorie and I have spent a small fortune bailing her out. So when she brought the thrice-divorced Mark home and told us' – he cleared his throat – '*this* was the man she wanted to marry, we knew there was no point arguing.'

Every guest was straining to catch his quiet words now. The smokers were poking their heads through the windows. Even the barman had paused.

'As we got to know Mark better, I had hoped we might come to understand what Monica sees in him.'

He stared down at his scrap of paper. The silence that followed was broken only by clattering from the kitchen and the occasional yell from the feral kids outside.

Finally, after the most agonising tumbleweed moment in the history of tumbleweed moments, he lifted his glass: 'To the bride and groom.'

'To the bride and groom,' repeated the guests.

'May God help them,' muttered Monica's dad.

And as the wine flowed, the atmosphere thawed and Dad wandered around, seeking shots of people at least pretending to enjoy themselves. Fingers crossed, the Salmonella en Croute appeared to be staying inside everyone who'd eaten it, and by the time the Black Forest gateau was served I had a little surge of hope it would be OK after all.

Oh ho ho, *no*.

With a *tinggg* of fork on glass, the best man stood up and the room instantly erupted in heckles. I had that sinking *he reckons he's a bit of a joker* feeling. By the time he'd finished, I'd almost chewed my knuckles to the bone.

He kicked off his speech with a joke about the bride that was so outrageously dirty my ears needed a tetanus booster. Mark the Groom grinned as his best friend proceeded to slur his way through a selection of lively anecdotes. Many of them involved the stag do. Most of them involved alcohol. All of them involved women who weren't Monica.

And just when I thought he'd reached peak awfulness, he proposed a toast.

'All that remains for me to say is raise your glasses to the happy couple. To Mark and . . . and . . . *Um*.'

Mum started frantically clapping, triggering the rest of the guests into action. Mark slapped his mate on the back. Poor '*Um*' flipped her veil over her face and gestured to the waiter for another bottle of wine.

When the DJ started, I thought the two families might link arms and start high-kicking to 'Come on Eileen', but they just continued to stare daggers at each other across the dance floor. Seriously, I'd been to funerals with more 'lol's.

Mark and Monica's budget hadn't stretched to the photo booth, so I collected empties to take my mind off the wedding and away from stray thoughts of Toby.

On my way to the recycling bins, I bumped into the groom coming out of the Gents, wiping his hands down his trousers.

'Daisy, isn't it?' he said, clasping my hand for far, far too long between his wet fingers.

'Yes it is! Congratulations.' I extracted my hand and pointed at the crate of empty bottles. 'I'd better, you know . . .'

'Of course,' he said. 'See you around.' And with a leery wink he slimed away and I ran into the Ladies. Ugh. I scrubbed my palms red raw, but not even a skin graft could erase that level of ick. With a grim smile, I wondered where Toby was when I *really* needed him.

I finally made it outside and there was Monica, leaning against a skip and sucking furiously on a cigarette, bridal make-up smudged into a Picasso portrait: Girl Who Has Made A Huge Mistake.

'You know,' she said conversationally, waving the glowing tip of her fag dangerously close to her veil, 'you know when your friends beg you not to do sh-sh-omething and you know they're right, but you don't want to admit you've made a mishtake?'

I held my breath. Swigging straight from a bottle of champagne, she mimed ear-chat with the hand holding the cigarette. Her bouffy updo wobbled like a hairy Weetabix.

She burped loudly. 'They shaid *don't marry him, Monica, he's a twat.*'

At least half a can, I reckoned. Maybe even three quarters. That's how much hairspray it'd take to hold a beehive of that magnitude. One stray spark and BOOM! her head would go off like a grenade.

'He promised me he'd change.' She took a last drag and ground the butt out with her heel. 'Yeah, right. I should've lishened to my friends. I hope you lishen to your friends. Friends are alwaysh right.'

'I will,' I said. 'I do. Monica, could I borrow your lighter, please?'

She handed it over absent-mindedly and I tucked it in my pocket. There'd be no ticking hair bombs on *my* watch, thank you very much.

'Are you a shingle girl?' she asked.

'Shingle? Um, yes, I am sh-single. I think.'

'I wish I was,' she said so sadly it made me want to find Mark and punch his cocky lights out.

I patted her arm. 'Now, Monica. Stay. Right. There.'

I dashed back into the hall, hoping to find Mum and instead spotted the groom talking intimately to a female guest. She was gazing up at him. He licked his lips and tucked a stray lock of hair behind her ear.

I saw that Monica had ignored my instruction and followed me back inside. She took one look at her new husband, grabbed the DJ's microphone and started wailing along to 'I Will Shurvive'. Mum went over and gently prised it out of her hand. Then, with the help of a bridesmaid, she coaxed her out of the hall and into a side room to sit down.

Mark and his revolting hands had vanished. As had the girl he'd been sliming them over.

After what felt like a hundred years, the last guests finally left and I went back to find Dad by the bar, as shell-shocked as any man would be who'd just witnessed a terrible accident.

'You know, Daze, the day me and your mum got married was the happiest day of my life,' he said, pulling at the knot to loosen his tie. 'Well, apart from when you and River came along, obviously.'

'*Obviously.*'

'Please promise me you will never, ever put our family through something like the car crash that happened here today.' He gestured round the room.

'Cross my heart and hope to die.' I said.

'How Monica's dad kept his hands off the groom is beyond me.' Dad shook his head. 'If that was your wedding, I'd have throttled him.'

'If that was my wedding, I'd have throttled myself,' I said.

'Oh well, it could've been worse,' Dad carried on heavily. 'At least no one died.'

As he spoke, Mr Quality Catering ambled past in his ancient, crusty chef's greys, his arms full of ancient, crusty cookware.

'Yet,' Dad added under his breath. 'No one has died *yet*.'

CHAPTER 18

If there were any fatalities we never got to hear about them. The morning after Officially the Worst Wedding Ever saw me loafing about the house in my scruffs, my hair in a messy ponytail, my face just in a mess.

I still hadn't heard a thing from Toby and that had me feeling part relieved, part ego-slapped. But mainly angry. Scaldingly, boilingly, explosively angry. We'd . . . I didn't know what the word was for breaking up with someone I didn't know if I was officially 'with'. We'd 'whatevered' over a stupid selfie I hadn't wanted to take in a restaurant I hadn't wanted to be in on a night out when I'd much rather have been in bed. It seemed ridiculously unfair. Also ridiculously . . . *intense*.

I was reading on the sofa, concentrating very hard on

the disaster zone that was the heroine's love life, when the doorbell rang.

'Daze, can you get that?' Mum shouted from the kitchen. 'I'm up to my elbows in hummus.'

'OK!' I shouted and put my book down. I'd been sitting in the same position so long, my leg had fallen asleep. Now pins and needles were coursing through it as I hopped and ow-ow-owed my way to open the front door.

Standing there, looking miserable, was Toby.

'Daisy . . .' he said, wedging his foot on the frame, 'I'm guessing you don't want to, but please talk to me. Please. I'm in a real mess.'

His usually groomed hair was sticking up in tufts and, as I gave him my finest lightsabre glare, he rubbed his hand across bleary puffy eyes. True: he was in a state.

But so what? Not my problem.

As I tried to close the door he put his hand out. 'Please,' he said again in a scratchy voice. 'Five minutes, that's all I'm asking.'

Mum came up behind me, drying her hands on a tea towel.

'Toby!' Don't stand there on the doorstep, come in. Have a cup of tea.'

'I'd love to,' he said, making a move to step inside.

Cheek! After what he'd done he was expecting to sit in my house and make polite conversation with my Mum?

Over my dead body.

Or, if Mum found out about him dumping me in a lay-by, Toby's.

'It's OK, we're going for a walk,' I said, nudging him back out with my elbow and slipping my feet into my Converse. Feet which were a (literal) painful reminder of Friday night.

We didn't speak until the front door was safely shut on Mum and I'd stalked halfway up the street.

'Daisy . . .'

It's hard to act the mature woman when you're wearing a Hello Kitty zombie T-shirt, but I did my best. Squared my shoulders, looked him in the eye. 'Why are you even here?'

'I'm so sorry,' he said.

'Yeah, well, it's a bit late for sorry,' I answered.

I was so mad, I could've shaken him. Sorry's not some magic rewind button: it's just a word and no words could change what had happened.

'Don't go, please,' he said, putting his hand out. 'At least give me another chance.'

'No.' I shrugged him off and folded my arms tightly across my chest. 'I gave you a chance *last* time you went off in a mood. You don't deserve another one now.'

'I didn't go off. I came back!' he said. 'In the car. You saw me.'

'So what?'

He had the nerve to sound annoyed. 'That's not very fair.'

'Not very fair?' I said, my voice going annoyingly high and squeaky. 'What about you? You dumped me by the side of the road in the middle of the night! I could've been murdered.'

'I wouldn't have let anything happen to you. I didn't go far, I could still see you. I just wanted to . . .' He tailed off, raking his hand through his messy hair. 'I don't know *what* I wanted to do. I saw you with that lad in the photo and I couldn't think straight.'

'Toby, you know what? You can explain all you like, it won't make any difference. It was one of the worst nights of my life.'

'I only drove a few metres. I would never have just left you there.'

'That makes it worse!' I could feel heat rising up my

cheeks. 'You must've known I was terrified. And it was raining.'

'I'm sorry,' he said again, a little haltingly. 'I did come back to get you, but you were already getting in the taxi.'

A man stopped to let his dog sniff a tree and we fell silent. The dog cocked its leg. We both pretended not to see.

'Oh, do come *on*, Roger,' snapped the man in a ridiculously posh voice, dragging the lead so the poor dog nearly fell over. Me and Toby caught each other's eye and I had to clench my poorly toes not to go hysterical at the weirdness of everything.

'Look,' said Toby quietly when they'd gone, 'if I could take it back, I would. All I can say is I'm sorry. I'm having a really hard time right now. Living with Jeff is doing my head in; my dad's on my case twenty-four seven.'

I closed my eyes and sighed. 'OK, it's sad your parents split up, but loads of people's parents get divorced.'

He shrugged. 'I know.'

'It's no excuse for treating me like dirt.'

'I know,' he said again, quietly staring down at the ground. 'Everything's falling apart. And it's all my fault.'

I looked at him. I didn't get him at all. He had taken

something with twinkly future potential and ruined it for both of us. It was beginning to feel like we were starring in our own teen movie. Except without enough of the fun, getting-to-know-you opening scenes. Nope, Toby had grabbed the remote and fast-forwarded us to the crap-that-makes-or-breaks-us sequence.

'So what do you think?' he said, eyeing me as if the script was already written and he knew my next move. 'Can we start again?'

The girl. The boy. And the misunderstanding forcing them apart.

What *was* my character's next move?

One look at his sorrowful expression and her heart skips a beat. Shining drops sparkle on his long dark lashes. His voice catches with regret as he steps closer. 'Daisy . . .'

Her thumb brushes away a single glimmering tear. He was wrong to dump her in a lay-by, but she can't bear those misery-filled eyes. Seeing his remorse, no words can do justice to her tumbled emotions.

No words?

Not true.

There were *many* words I could've used to describe myself at that precise moment. Pushover wasn't one of them.

Heartbeat unskipped, tear unbrushed, words unsaid, I turned away from him.

'I'm going home,' I said. And as I walked off, I didn't look back.

Toby called my name out once, but I didn't hear any footsteps as I trudged up the path and the doorbell didn't ring again.

My phone pinged a text as I got in. Ayesha.

How's things? xxx

Just seen Toby. Told him it's definitely over xx

Sad face and thumbs-up emojis. **I think you're doing the right thing xx**

You in later? Can I come round? Really need to talk Xxx

She didn't answer right away, but that was OK. I had an important task and it needed to be done quickly or I'd bottle it. A series of quick sharp cuts to make.

Contacts first. Scroll down, scroll down. Toby's name. Delete. Next up, messages. Delete all.

Felt a bit wobbly, but I knew Ayesha was right. Cutting Toby off completely was the only way.

I'd just clicked on Delete All Call Logs when the phone buzzed in its demonic waspy way: not a text, but Ayesha ringing. As soon as I picked up, the way she breathed in sharply told me straightaway there was Bad News coming.

'Sorry, Daze, I can't do today. A bunch of us, er, are seeing Matt this afternoon.'

'Eh?'

'And we're going to meet Rosa. Sorry.'

I didn't realise this actually happened outside books, but her words made me flinch. More came tumbling down the phone, but I was still digesting 'meet Rosa'.

Meet.

Rosa.

'So how about we do something tomor—'

'Whoa, hang on,' I cut in. 'Go back. What do you mean "seeing Matt"?'

'He's over at his dad's; they're having a barbecue. We're all going round . . .' She hesitated. 'He flew in last night. With Rosa.'

I let that sink in.

At this precise moment, Matt, the boy I'd thought I'd be with forever, was less than two miles away, grilling sausages with another girl.

'Which means I won't be in, sorry. I'm really —'

'Wait, wait,' I interrupted. 'Who's "we"?'

'Oh, um, me, Tom, Beth, Shaney, Jasmin, the football lads . . . you know, the usual St Mary's lot. Everyone.'

I let that sink in too.

Since when did Jasmin start being one of the usual lot? Since when did I *stop*?

'*Riiiight,*' I said. 'How come no one told me?'

'We didn't want you getting upset. You know, with Rosa being there.'

'Rosa? I don't care about *Rosa,*' I lied. 'When will you get it? I am OVER Matt. I couldn't care less who he sees or where he goes.'

'All right, Daisy,' said Ayesha calmly.

Anger surged through me like lava or gunpowder or . . . some other explosive substance. 'Stop patronising me!' I said. 'You're always patronising me!'

'I'm really sorry you feel like that. Why don't I call you later when —?'

'Still doing it!' I yelled. 'Still patronising!' And I put the phone down.

For the rest of the afternoon, when I wasn't crying, I was obsessively techno-stalking Matt and eating unhealthy foodstuffs until I started crying again.

In between, I texted Ayesha to say sorry. She

answered straight back with **You did the right thing, but if you need to talk about Toby we can definitely do it soon xxx**

Balls. Where was a time machine when I needed one?

I wanted to rewind to the day Matt left and tell him we could make it work, like long-distance Megan and Ben had. Create myself an alternative future where I *didn't* leave St Mary's/fall out with my friends/get usurped by Rosa and the Amazing Jasmin. A future where I wouldn't be well and truly screwed up by Toby.

Failing that, I wanted to lie under a duvet with a family pack of Jaffa Cakes, watching box sets until someone with more technical ability than me invented time travel.

The expensive black dress glared snootily down at me from the wardrobe door, labels still on. I stuck my tongue out at it, then stuffed three Jaffa Cakes in at once. Ha. Take *that*, dress.

Nothing tastes as good as skinny feels. Wasn't that what people said?

Total bollocks. Nothing tastes as good as *food*.

I had to give the dress back, I knew that. After all, there was no way I'd be at Tom's eighteenth now, with or without Toby.

What was wrong with me? I was the love anti-Midas: everything I touched turned to crap.

And when *that* thought struck me, I put the Jaffa Cakes down and had yet another cry.

CHAPTER 19

You did the right thing.

Ayesha's words echoed in my head as the bus made its way to college, the dull Tuesday sky matching my sludge-tinged mood exactly. Not a glimmer of sunshine, just grey, grey, grey as I held the bag with the dress on my knee.

I'd faked a headache to stay home yesterday, but I couldn't chicken out of facing Toby forever. I knew I'd done the *right* thing walking away from his apology. But being right wasn't the same as being happy. And all the rightness in the world couldn't lift the gloom as I stared out of the window.

Walking through the foyer, I had a swoosh of stomach-churning déjà vu. But there was no unpredictable romantic hero leaning against a pillar. And I didn't see him in the canteen when I queued for coffee. Lessons came and went, but I may as well have stayed in bed for all I learned.

ASBO lifted now, I tried the library in my afternoon free period, but he wasn't there either. So, with Colin keeping a close and lushly fringed eye on me, I sent an email that had echoes of the first I'd ever sent. To the point but friendly:

Are you in college? I've got your dress with me to give back. D.

I was logging out when my phone flashed: **Big fountain at the Trafford Centre after you've finished?**

Hmmm.

I could meet up, call him a selection of names, hand over the dress, come back home, get changed, go to footie training, go home, lie on the bed feeling sorry for myself.

Plan.

By some miracle I got to the meeting place early. Even so, Toby was earlier.

I hesitated in the entrance, watching him sitting

there, lost in his moody, broody thoughts as he stared at the spouting dolphins. His long legs were stretched out straight in front and, as I got closer, he pushed his floppy hair off his forehead. He was born to play the part of 'handsome sad boy sitting on a bench'.

He dumped you in a lay-by, I reminded myself as I marched towards him.

'Hi.' I held the bag out. 'Here it is. Um, it's still got the labels on and I put the receipt in the bottom, so . . .'

He made no move to take it as I tailed off. I lowered my arm so the bag brushed his knees, 'Hello Toby, the dress?'

'Can we go for something to eat?' he said, continuing his morose dolphin-gazing. 'I don't want things to be awkward between us.'

'Um . . .'

'Daisy,' he said, straightening up to look up at me, 'it's important we sort this out. I don't want us to spend the year cutting each other dead in the corridor.' He pushed his shoulders back as he stood up. 'Plus, I'm starving.'

He looked me right in the eyes then and I don't know what swung it. Maybe his weary voice or the thought of college awkwardness, or of Matt and Rosa, or the fact that he mentioned food. Whatever it was, within five minutes I found myself sharing a table with a toasted mozzarella ciabatta and a boy I'd sworn never to speak to again.

'How come you weren't in college today?' I asked, taking the sandwich out of its paper bag.

He leaned back in his chair and exhaled loudly. 'Short version is Mum and Jeff have set the wedding date, Dad's found out and he's . . . how can I put it?'

'Not invited?'

He gave a short, humour-free laugh. '*Definitely* not invited. "Taken it hard" might be a good way of phrasing it.' He shook his head. 'Gone crazy-ape batshit might be another. So I've got that to deal with and now I've totally screwed things up with you.'

'Ungh,' I non-answered. I'd been rendered speechless by the ciabatta. It was like chewing through a flip-flop.

'I've been meaning to tell you about this girlfriend I had back home,' said Toby slowly, crumpling the paper bag from his sandwich into a ball. 'I thought it might make you understand.'

'Ungh?'

'Yeah.' He flattened the bag out again. 'Rhiannon. I was gutted when we split up.'

I chewed and nodded. Yep, break-up angst. I understood that.

'Whenever I felt crap, she could make me laugh my way out of it. She was great.'

As he went on, the spooky parallel with me and Matt was hard to ignore. Toby and Rhiannon had been the Posh and Becks of their school until he'd moved away.

Toby was now flattening the bag's creases with his thumbnail. 'That's how I got the car,' he said. 'Mum bought it so I could drive back to see Rhi.'

But 'Rhi' started making excuses not to see him.

'In the end, a guy from school told me she'd starting seeing my so-called best mate,' Toby said in a low voice. 'He admitted it'd been going on since I left. I was in pieces. Couldn't speak to anyone, stopped going to rugby, stopped going to *college*. That's how I've ended up repeating the year.'

He tilted his head back, exhaled loudly, then abruptly sat up straight. 'The stupid thing was, I was the one who asked him to keep an eye on her.'

'That's awful.' I put my hand over his. I knew *exactly* how that felt: the betrayal, the pain, the having your dreams crushed to atoms. Yep, all of it.

'Thank you,' he said, curling his fingers round mine

and leaning forward. 'But that's not even the worst bit.'

As he sketched out the events leading up to the 'worst bit', I let my rubber-filled ciabatta grow cold. I needed my mouth on standby for *gasping*, *dropping wide open* and *lifting hand in shock to* purposes.

Whoa.

'Let me get this straight,' I said when he'd finished and I'd kind of got my head round it. 'Your mum's boyfriend Jeff is Rhiannon's *dad*?'

'Yes.'

'And he and your mum started an affair when you went on a skiing holiday.'

'Yep, both families, Andorra.' He half laughed. 'Not much snow that year.'

'And now Jeff and your mum are getting married, meaning that your ex-girlfriend . . .'

'Who two-timed me with my best mate, hates my mum's guts and refuses to speak to her own dad . . .'

'. . . is going to be your stepsister.' I finished up for him.

It took me every molecule of self-restraint not to add *EastEnders* drums on the end. *Doof doof doof . . .*

'Yeah, my life is a soap opera,' said Toby the mind-reader.

He took his phone out and thumb-flicked through

the pictures. 'That's Rhi,' he said, handing it to me.

Wtf? It was like seeing a picture of myself maybe a stone lighter with a tan and better hair.

Spooky.

We had the exact same long ash-blonde hair, but whereas mine went heavy metal-mosh pit at the merest hint of moisture, hers was silky sleek even on a ski slope. Her eyes sparkled and she was laughing uproariously at something, showing a set of Tipp-Ex-white teeth.

Of course, other details were different. Her chin was more rounded and her eyes were brown not blue. And I don't ski. Or paint my teeth with correction fluid. But the resemblance was obvious, like seeing myself photoshopped.

What was that emotion surging through me? Oh yeah, that's it: totally freaked-outness.

I kept waiting for Toby to comment on the weird similarity between us, but he didn't. He'd drifted off back through the mists of time to Rhiannon's two-timing.

'I was constantly on Facebook, Instagram, you name it. I couldn't leave it alone,' he said, putting his phone back in his pocket. 'Hours and hours. I was getting as mental as my dad. Ended up deleting all my accounts.'

He pushed his uneaten sandwich away, took both of my hands in his and pulled me towards him until our faces were almost touching.

'So I'm not asking you to forgive me, Daisy, because I know I don't deserve it. What I did was terrible. But I just wanted to explain where it came from, you know, the trust thing. And that I'm sorry; I know you didn't do anything wrong. And to tell you that, please, I want you to keep the dress.'

The dress. The party. Ayesha.

I jumped up, checking the time on my phone. Ooops.

'Oh God, I've got football. I need to go,' I said, panicking.

Toby got up too. 'Come on, I'll drive you there.'

'I need my kit and it's at home,' I said. 'Ayesha is going to totally kill me.'

'It's OK,' he said. 'I'll take you home to fetch it and then drop you off at the training ground, yeah?'

I hesitated, caught somewhere between *I need a lift* and *last time I got in your car I had a near-death experience*.

Yes, no, yes, no.

'That'd be brilliant,' I said. 'Thanks.'

*

And that's how, twenty-five minutes later, I'd been home to swap the bag with the dress for the one with my kit. Toby's tales of family nightmares kept on coming in the car. With parents as awesome as mine it was easy to forget that 'home' wasn't a happy word for everyone. And by the time we turned off by the training ground, he'd managed to press my pity buttons big time.

We pulled up at exactly the same time as Ayesha arrived.

'Hi, Ayesha,' called Toby through the open window as I got out. She cut him dead with a filthy glare.

'*Daisy?*' she said.

Toby raised his eyebrows. Then he reached his hand out of the car and caught mine, 'I'll ring you later, babes.' And he drove out of the car park, leaving me to face the wrath of Ayesha Warrior Princess alone.

'Tell me I did not just see you getting out of that boy's car,' she said, hands on hips. 'Tell me you wouldn't be that dumb.'

'He just gave me a lift, that's all.' I knew I sounded defensive. 'I wouldn't have made it here on time otherwise.'

'You promised you were going to, and I quote, "never speak to Toby Smith again",' she reminded me.

'So did you *mime* your way into accepting a lift? Use *sign language*? Send him a *note*?'

'I can't avoid him; we go to the same college. Anyway, I wasn't going to, but then we had a long conversation and I . . . and I kind of get why he did what he did.'

To say she didn't take that well would be something of an understatement.

'*What?!*'

I looked down at the ground, searching for an explanation that wouldn't sound totally lame. But the ground held no answers. 'He's really, really sorry,' I said, lamely. 'He's having a really hard time.'

She looked at me like I'd just grown two heads. 'Daisy, can you hear yourself? He dumped you by the side of the road in the middle of the night. It doesn't matter if he spends the rest of his life force-feeding you diamonds, he put you in DANGER.'

'It was a stupid misunderstanding,' I said, surprising myself with how much I actually believed that now. 'Anyway, I'm not saying I'm going to be his girlfriend, just that I kind of get why it happened.' The sound of balls being booted drifted over the wall. 'Come on, we're missing the warm up.'

Her face flipped through several emotions in quick

succession before finally settling on furious.

'We're not going anywhere until you promise me you're not going to see Toby again.'

'Oh, come on, Ayesha, you're the one who told me to go out with him in the first place!'

She flapped her mouth open and shut in cartoon disbelief. '*Noooo*, I told you to have some fun. I didn't say go forth and date a control freak.'

'He isn't a control freak,' I protested turning the volume up to match hers. 'He's just got trust issues.'

I thought Ayesha's head would explode. 'Let me tell you who else had "trust issues" – Psycho Dan. This is exactly how he started, Daisy. Checking on my mum, turning up when she was out, going mad if she spoke to anyone else. You're on a slippery slope and you need to get off it right now.'

'Well, what about Shaney?' I snapped.

'What's Shaney got to do with anything?'

'Well, when I was going, *Beth, step away from the illiterate schoolgirl botherer,* you were like, *No, give him a chance.*' I put on a whingy voice. '*Everyone has teething troubles, cut poor Shaney some slack, blah blah blah.* So why aren't you doing the same for Toby, eh?'

'Teething troubles? We were discussing how Beth

could learn to cope with her boyfriend's obsessive cleaning habit!' she shouted. 'Toby DUMPED YOU AT THE SIDE OF THE ROAD.'

'He only *pretended* to drive off,' I insisted. 'It's not that big a deal.'

'Oh, get real, Daisy! You could've been abducted, attacked, anything. It's hardly the same as bulk-buying Toilet Duck, is it?'

From inside the ground, cheers and shouts told us that training had started, but neither of us moved. My heart was beating fast. Ayesha's mouth had opened, revving up for more. But it was my turn.

'Look,' I said more quietly, 'I know you see these things in a certain way because of what happened with your mum, but honestly, Toby's nothing like Dan. He's had a rough time and his head's a bit messed up, that's all. I really think you're overreacting.'

'God, Daze,' she said, coming up close to put her hands on my shoulders, 'listen to yourself making excuses for him. They're not *trust* issues, They're *twat* issues. It's not right he kicked you out of his car. It's not right he gets you to send him all those selfies. And before you say anything –' I had my mouth open to protest '– before you say it's because he loves your beautiful face or he loves nans or whatever, you must know it's bollocks. He's checking up on you.'

Lishen to your friends, the ghost of Monica's voice warned.

Ayesha continued, softly now. 'You don't need him, Daze. There's loads of other guys you could go out with. Or not. Be single, be anything, just don't start something with *him*. If you don't end it now, I guarantee it will be a disaster. *Guarantee* it. It's Rule number 1, Daisy and, I'm sorry, but Toby is definitely a twat.'

I put my hands up and pushed Ayesha off. Thoughts and feelings that had been bubbling for the past few weeks shot to the surface.

I sighed loudly. 'For God's sake, stop going on about the stupid Rules. We're not in Year 7 now. And anyway, you are such a total hypocrite.'

She reached out to touch my arm. Tried to get a word in, but I shouted her down.

'I saw your posts on Facebook.' I got the whingy voice back out. '*Hope Rosa has a great trip, Matt! Bring Rosa to Tom's eighteenth to make Daisy really feel like crap, Matt!* And then, THEN you go to his barbecue with your own perfect boyfriend and everyone else except me so you can all talk about how lucky Matt is to have met

Rosa. So go on, which part of *Can't wait to meet Rosa!* is following the Rules?

'You need to calm down,' she said.

I think I may have actually stamped my foot. 'Stop patronising me! *You're* the one who's paranoid, imagining stuff. Yes, Toby made a mistake on Friday. Well, at least I understand *why* he did it. I've got no idea why you and Beth have stabbed me in the back. Making out nothing is more important than friendship when you clearly don't give a toss about how I feel.'

Panting now and really quite sweaty, I inhaled deeply before hurling my final clincher: 'We're not eleven and we're not in some secret girly club. So why don't you just shut up with your stupid Rules, leave me alone and go and marry *Jasmin*.'

CHAPTER 20

Marry Jasmin.

Clear the mantelpiece, Mum: if there's a category for Most Immature Piece of Unscripted Dialogue at the Oscars this year, we're going to need the space.

Ayesha's expression suggested she was trying to work out 'marry Jasmin' as I'd stormed out of the car park.

She'd called after me, 'Daisy, don't go.'

'Leave me alone,' I shouted back.

Never in my life had I argued with Ayesha this badly. We'd had the odd disagreement of course; all friends do. But none had left me sick and shaking before.

The Weather Gods had laid on a spectacular autumn sunset for my long walk home, but torrential rain or thunder would have suited my mood better. Hail even. Yeah, a few golf balls of ice smacking me, that would work. What use was this sci-fi light show of purples and peaches and golds?

As I trudged on, it only reminded me there was a whole universe out there and I, Daisy Green, was a lonely speck of dust on an insignificant rock whirling through eternal darkness towards . . . nothing.

'You're back early,' said Mum as me and the crushing pointlessness of my existence entered the kitchen. 'How was football?'

The table was stacked high with paperwork and she was jabbing at her calculator as she spoke. From the sound of it, River was watching telly in the front room.

'Yeah, fine,' I lied. 'Where's Dad?'

'Last-minute corporate awards thing. Their photographer's sick, so she rang Dad. But he could do with an extra pair of hands.'

'You or me?' I said and she beamed.

'That's the spirit. Thanks, love, we weren't sure if you had plans.'

'No plans,' I yawned.

Mum yawned back and stretched like a cat. She flapped her hand at the scatter of invoices and receipts. 'I could do with getting out to be honest. I've been doing wed-min all day.' She started slipping the paperwork into different-coloured folders. 'And I'm pleased to say we can seriously think about getting a part-timer.'

I was at the sink, filling a pint glass. 'That's great.'

She stood up, 'So, if you can think of anyone, let me know. Now are you sure you're OK to babysit?'

I thumbs-upped as I downed the water in one long gulp.

Cosying up on the sofa watching a DVD with my lovely little brother was one of my favourite things to do, so when the doorbell rang twenty minutes before the end of *Frozen*, I wasn't in any rush to get up.

'Who is it?' asked River.

'No idea,' I answered, pressing pause as I heaved myself off the sofa.

Ayesha? Toby? Some random pivot-eyed weirdo offering to tarmac the drive? It rang again. 'All right, all right. Keep your wig on,' I muttered.

There on the doorstep was Matt.

Matt.

MATT.

You know how it feels when you see your ex-boyfriend unexpectedly and you realise that finally, after months of pining and missing him, you're completely over it and seeing him is a total non-event?

Well, I didn't. I had to lean against the door frame to catch my breath. I nearly passed out.

'Hi,' he said, almost shyly, 'I wanted to ring, but . . .'

'*Hufrf* –' I cleared my throat. 'Hi, er, yeah.'

A silence fell between us in which neither of us mentioned that I'd blocked his number.

'You look well,' he said, leaning forward to kiss me on the cheek.

'You too,' I said, but only one of us was telling the truth. It felt as if every drop of blood had drained from my face and I had to clasp my hands together to hide the shaking.

'I was wondering –' he began, when River came barrelling down the hallway.

'Maaaaattttttty!'

'Mate!' said Matt, an expression of genuine delight on his face as he picked River up and swung him round. 'I have missed you, little buddy.'

He put River down and they went immediately into a complicated fist bump/handshake ritual that ended in them both giggling.

'Can we go play football, can we?' River was scampering round Matt's legs.

'You'll have to ask Daisy,' said Matt, patting him on the head.

River tugged on my skirt. 'Can we? Can we?'

'It's pitch-dark, Riv,' I pointed out. 'Maybe we should just get Matt to come in.'

And with that, I added the final twist to my rollercoaster of a day.

We watched the rest of the film. Well, Matt and River did. My head was a long way from Arendelle.

'It's way past your bedtime,' I said, lifting River up when the credits rolled. 'No arguments. Say night night.'

'Can Matty read my story? Please?'

'Please?' Matt said, mimicking River's little boy cuteness. How could I say no?

Matt's Gruffalo voice and River's giggles filtered down as I tidied up in the kitchen and it made me smile, remembering all the times I'd heard them before. Happy days.

Then Matt was back downstairs and it was just me and him.

'*I'm the scariest creature in this wood*,' he growled from the hall, obviously temporarily forgetting we were being awkward with each other.

'He really misses you,' I said. *I really miss you.*

We stood there for a few seconds, not speaking until he said, 'Is the kettle on then?'

I filled it and got the teabags out while he sat in his usual spot at our kitchen table, which was as usual hidden under a layer of magazines, toys and random bits of paper.

'That's one thing about Spain,' he said, rolling one of River's plastic cars around a coaster. 'You can't get a decent cup of tea anywhere.'

I made it the right way: milk, one sugar. He lifted the chipped *Meat is Murder* mug and took a sip. 'Lovely,' he said.

'How's the bar going?' I asked, pulling up a chair. 'Things working out?'

'Yeah, better than Mum expected really. She loves it. The sun and the lifestyle and everything.'

'And are you enjoying it?' I said. 'You look well on it.'

He smiled. 'Yeah, it's good, Spain. Well, you know, there's good and bad sides like anywhere.'

'And . . . Rosa? How's that going?'

There. I'd said it.

He looked down at his mug.

Uncomfortable pause.

'Yeah, her mate's on an exchange at the uni so

277

she's staying with her in town.' He lifted the mug to his lips. 'Ayesha mentioned you'd started seeing someone from college. Toby, is it?'

'What did she say about him?' I asked, instantly alert.

'Um, that was it really.'

More uncomfortable silence.

Then, 'I was think—'

'You know, me and Ros—'

We both spoke and stopped at the same time. 'Go on,' said Matt.

'Doesn't matter,' I said, standing up. 'I'd better check on River anyway.'

He drained the last of his tea and handed the mug over. 'Good to see you, Daze.'

'Yeah, same,' I said as we went into the hall.

'So, you going to Tom's party?' he said at the door.

'Yeah.' *No. Maybe.*

We had a hug measuring twenty out of ten on the Awkward Hugs Scale and then he was gone.

And it wasn't until I was in bed, replaying the whole conversation, that I realised I hadn't let him tell me about Rosa.

CHAPTER 21

The teacher let us out of English five minutes early, leaving just enough time for a quick mirror sesh before I went off to meet Toby. I had my phone out as I made my way to the toilets. My stomach sank: still nothing from Ayesha.

By the time Friday came round, my head was in a complete mess. When I thought about Ayesha, it felt as though I'd swallowed a rock. Beth was frantic about us, I knew, and Tom had texted to check I was still on for the party.

I was, I told him. And I was bringing Toby.

I pushed the door open and saw Badger's friend Gemma by the sinks, blotting her red lipstick on a tissue.

'Hi, Daisy,' she said with a big smile. 'How's things?'

'Yeah, good. I LOVE your jacket.' Corduroy, fitted

and with an amazing cut-apple print. I reached out to touch the lapel. 'I've never seen one like that before. It's gorgeous.'

'Got it from eBay. I altered it myself to fit and –' she opened it up to reveal a green silk lining printed with apple cores '– added this.'

Wow. Mum-standard work (no higher praise), technically perfect *and* creative. It sparked a little Something Borrowed light bulb in my head.

Just then a toilet flushed and Brittany appeared beside us in the mirror. She looked Gemma up and down and gave a little snort as she turned on the tap.

'Sorry, I missed that, Brittany. What did you say?' I said.

'Me?' she said with fake innocence. 'Oh, nothing.'

'Right, see you later, Daisy,' said Gemma.

'Yeah, definitely,' I answered, locking myself in a cubicle. When I came out, Brittany was still admiring herself from different angles in the mirror, pushing her hair up, then smoothing it back down. I washed my hands, smoothed down my own hair and, without a word, strode into the corridor to the sound of her witchy cackle.

As I got near the canteen, she overtook me, still snorting little giggles to herself. *God, she could not be more annoy—*

A hand on my arm. Gemma. 'Your skirt,' she whispered. 'It's all . . .' She mimed tucking something down the back of her tights. I quickly adjusted it, feeling the swish of material as it took up its rightful position over my arse.

Too late though.

Burning with rage, I made my way through the canteen to Donkey Corner. 'Hey, gorgeous,' Toby said, reaching up to give me a kiss. 'Move up, Brittany, let Daisy in.'

Her smirky bitchface told me everything I needed to know. What a cow.

Toby held my hand and smiled. Next to us, the boneheaded donkeys were discussing their plans for the weekend in their typically sophisticated and mature fashion.

'Yeah,' said Jozz, 'so who's up for trying to get in at Bag a Slag tonight?'

'Please tell me it's not really called that,' I whispered to Toby.

'Over twenty-fives night,' he mouthed back.

'Come on, lads,' pleaded Jozz, apparently oblivious to his girlfriend's presence. 'It'll be a right laugh. Cheap beer. Proper tunes. More birds than you can shake a stick at.'

Ugh. I was sure Jozz had 'shaken his stick' at many unfortunate women since he hit puberty. And although 99.9 per cent of them undoubtedly consisted of pixels and/or imagination, for a split second I almost felt sorry for Brittany.

Then I remembered she let me stroll through the canteen with my skirt tucked in my knickers and the sorry feeling went away.

'Not that I'll be on the hunt,' he added, sliding his hand up Brittany's leggings. 'I've got my own bird.'

Bird? I couldn't help it, I tutted and gave an exasperated eye roll. In return, she shot me a death-ray glare that I successfully blanked.

'Count me out, mate,' said Toby. 'We've got plans. It's Daisy's mate's eighteenth.'

Quicker than you could say 'mate's boyfriend's actually', Jozz was in there, sounding way too interested for my liking. 'Party? Where?'

'Will there be strippers?' said Mozz, shifting in his seat, presumably to relieve some naked lady angst in his pants.

Noooo! The voice of Ayesha deafened me with a banshee wail. I'd pinned my hopes on the party making her realise she needed to give Toby the same chance she'd given Shaney. If he turned up with a herd of sexist donkeys in tow, she'd never speak to me again, never mind Toby.

'I'm not even sure they'll let me in,' Toby was saying with a smirk. 'Daisy's mates all hate me.'

'Of course they don't hate you!' I lied, shifting my knees to one side to let another couple of donkeys squeeze past.

'Well, whatshername certainly does.' Toby leaned back with his legs spread out.

'Who?'

'Ayesha, is it? The hairy footballer one.' He clasped his hands behind his head. 'Moshi Monster.'

The donkeys hee-hawed and Toby grinned. I whipped round to face him. 'That's a horrible thing to say. She's not hairy.'

Toby held his palms up. 'Just an observation.'

'Well, it's not nice,' I said, adding, 'and not true.'

Toby laughed. 'Sorry, but I don't suppose she's been saying "nice" things about me either.'

Which was fair enough, but hardly the point.

The uncomfortable pause that followed was broken by Bozz, a boy so dim he'd struggle to pick himself out in a line-up, asking, 'Why would anyone want to shake a stick at a bird?'

With the Bozz-bashing banter well under way, Gemma and Badger arrived hand in hand and looking slightly uncomfortable.

'Hi,' I said gratefully, shifting up on the bench to make room. 'Come and sit down.'

'No, it's OK,' said Badger quickly, taking a step back. 'We're going into town. Just wondered if you fancied coming?'

I'd picked up my bag and was already sliding out when Toby stopped me, his arm tight round my shoulder. 'Daisy, we don't have time. We need to sort out what we're doing for the party.'

'OK,' said Gemma, waving at me. 'Another time.'

Badger nodded. 'See you at the wedding then.'

'Oh, right.' I dropped my rucksack on the floor. 'See you tomorrow.'

I watched them head towards the exit, feeling Toby's arm clutching my shoulder and wondered how my vision of an exciting new start at college had turned into this.

Then Bozz's puzzled voice broke through my thoughts. 'What's this about going to see hairy strippers?'

And the Bozz-bashing braying revved up another gear. *

'Tell Ayesha I've put the candles and the matches in the green bag,' Dad was saying. 'And tell her not to light them too early or the wax'll run down and wreck the icing.'

'Will do,' I promised, only half listening. It had just gone eight and I was lifting the front-room curtain for the tenth time in as many minutes. This time though Toby's black mini was just pulling up outside.

'OK, I'm off,' I said. My Docs watched forlornly from the shoe rack as I squashed my feet into the way-too-high sandals.

'Don't forget your key,' said Mum, dropping it inside my handbag. She tilted her head to one side, pursed her lips then smoothed back my hair. 'Say happy birthday to Tom for me.'

This was it. The biggest, best party of the year. Weeks of planning. My closest friends would be there. *Matt* would be there.

And I was dreading it.

Toby nodded approvingly as I tottered out to the car. 'I told you that dress would be perfect.'

'Thanks,' I said and clambered in.

It didn't take long to drive to the venue. When I caught sight of the glamorous, sophisticated girl reflected in the mirrored foyer I could hardly recognise myself.

'Daisy,' said Tom, coming up to greet me with a kiss. 'You look lovely. And Toby.' He stuck his hand out. 'All right, mate?'

'Happy birthday,' I said. 'Is Ayesha about? I need to give her . . .' I lifted the box.

I didn't imagine the fractional hesitation before he answered me. 'She was . . .' He craned his neck through the open door. 'Yeah, there she is in front of that big mirror. By the table with the presents on.'

'Shall I go to the bar then?' said Toby, looking round. The lights were dappling his white shirt with colour and I had to speak up over the music. 'Yeah, great. Can I have a . . . whatever. Anything, please.'

'Of course you can.' He grabbed me round the waist and pulled me close, speaking right in my ear. 'You are so gorgeous tonight, I can't keep my hands off you.'

Over his shoulder, I watched Ayesha taking a brightly coloured parcel from someone. I drew myself out of Toby's grasp.

'See you back here in a minute then,' I said.

Ayesha was stacking the gift-wrapped packages as I neared the table. In her pink silk halter-neck and with her hair left natural, she was beautiful. She looked up and gave me a subdued smile.

'Hi, Daisy,' she said quietly. 'Thanks for coming. Where's . . .?'

'Toby? He's gone to the bar,' I said quickly. 'Here.' I added my present to the pile and carefully placed the cake box on the table. 'Dad said not to light the candles too soon.'

She laughed. 'Don't worry. Your mum sent mine a text. The icing is safe. Did you go to footie?'

'Nah, didn't have time,' I said.

'I wasn't sure if you'd make it tonight if you got a wedding tomorrow and you're, you know, busy.' She stacked and then restacked a couple of boxes as she spoke.

'We've got a girl from college doing a trial day tomorrow. Gemma.' I took the paper bag with the candles and the matches out, laid it on the table. 'There's the, um . . .'

'Cheers,' she said. 'And that's good news, about the wedding. Should take some of the stress off.'

There was a pause. I unfastened my cardigan. Straightened the candles, twice, and made sure the lid was down properly on the cake box while *Rule #7 Boyfriends are the icing, girlfriends are the cake,* bounced round my head.

I'd come so close to losing Beth. How could I let another boy mess up my friendship with Ayesha?

I took a deep breath. 'I didn't know whether you'd want me here,' I said. 'You know, after . . . Tuesday '

'Of course I want you here,' she said simply.

I waved my hand at the pillars and in the direction of the bar. 'The decorations look great,' I said, 'and so do you.'

'You too. Nice dress. Is it new?'

I smoothed my hands down the skirt. 'It's the one Toby bought me.'

Pause. The Toby-shaped elephant in the room stood between us, but at least we were still trying. She bit her lip. 'Look, about Toby. You were right. I shouldn't have said what I did. As long as you're happy, then that's all that matters.' She froze, staring at the door behind me. 'Daisy, just so you know, Matt's just arrived.'

The whole room was reflected in the mirror and, as I turned my head slightly, I saw Matt illuminated by a spotlight. And there was Rosa. No other word for it: she was *stunning*.

I took a breath so deep it must've sucked half the air out of the room. I was almost expecting to see oxygen-starved people flapping and gasping on the floor. But no, there was only Matt and Rosa headed this way, gift-wrapped parcels in their hands. 'Only' Matt and Rosa.

'Oh *Goddd*,' I muttered.

Ayesha patted my hand, whispered, 'It'll be fine.'

On the plus side, at least Matt wasn't holding up a placard that read 'This is Rosa, look how unbelievably gorgeous she is.'

Then again, he didn't need one.

'Hello, hello,' he went, with forced cheeriness. After three years together, I recognised every tone his voice had. He leaned in, gave Ayesha a kiss on both cheeks, hesitated, then did the same to me.

He had one hand on the small of Rosa's back as he gestured at me with the other. 'Daisy, this is Rosa who works at my mum's bar. Rosa this is Daisy.'

From her glossy tamed curls to her petite, sandalled feet, she was perfect. When she said, 'Daisy, I've heard so much about you,' her English was flawless. Of course it was.

'Nice to meet you,' I said as we air-kissed. She smelled of sunshine and it made me want to cry. Over her shoulder I saw Toby striding towards us with the drinks. And suddenly I desperately, desperately wanted to be somewhere, anywhere else.

With a hasty 'bye' I scuttled off. Catching Toby's arm, I steered him over to the other side of the room.

'Who's that lad?' he said, his face set like stone.

Oh God, not now. 'My ex-boyfriend.'

'Right.' He narrowed his eyes and carried on staring at them while my stomach squirmed. Then *mood-flip* he smiled. 'Where's the food then?'

I let out the breath I'd been holding and followed him to the buffet.

Matt. Here. With Rosa. I considered this as I picked up a spring roll with the tongs and laid it next to the samosas already on my plate. Spearing a second chicken drumstick with my fork I became aware of Toby's eyes on me. He flicked his gaze from me to my plate, then to my fork, then back to my face before arching his eyebrows.

'What?' I said defensively.

'I never said a word,' he replied, eyes wide.

As long as you're happy, Ayesha had said and I dropped the drumstick on to my plate without a word.

Matt and Rosa were chatting with Shaney and Beth now. Shaney said something I couldn't hear and when they all burst out laughing, Matt did that thing he always did where he literally bent over with his hand over his mouth in hysterics. I smiled.

'Why do you keep looking at him?'

Ack. Quickly, I turned to Toby and plastered on an even bigger smile. 'Let's go and sit down over there.' And as quickly as the tottering shoes would let me, I headed towards one of the tables.

Jasmin and a few other girls were there, blatantly gawping at Toby who was acting the part of incredibly gorgeous, tight T-shirt wearing boy to perfection. And of course he'd switched his charm on full power and pretty soon ours was the table everyone was gravitating towards.

So the night perked up for a while at least. Toby laughed and talked and draped his arm casually along the back my chair. And if he was still brooding about Matt, he hid it well.

After a while I untangled myself. Or tried to.

'Where are you off to?' he said, catching my arm.

'Loo,' I answered. 'Won't be a minute.'

Downstairs was deserted and I was in no rush to get back. I finally got a break from pretending to be enjoying myself. I swept on some bronzer, freshened my lip-gloss, brushed my hair, adjusted the Belly Constrictors. *When did I turn in to someone who'd rather be in the toilets than at the party?* I wondered as I steeled myself to go back upstairs.

And there was Matt, leaning on the banister.

'Hi,' he said.

I stopped dead. 'Hi.'

The sound of music punctuated with laughter drifted down to us. Seeing Matt right in front of me, a surge of misery and longing flooded me. My throat ached.

'Are you having a good time?' he said.

I nodded, lying, not trusting myself to speak.

'You look totally beautiful.'

With a horrified lurch I realised I was going to cry. I nodded again, but I could feel my lips trembling.

Matt stepped closer and put his hand on my arm. 'Daze, you OK?' I pressed my lips together and blinked hard.

'Daisy, what's wrong?'

His voice was suddenly very close to my ear and the next thing I knew, Matt's familiar arms were around me and my cheek was resting on his warm chest.

'Hey,' he whispered into my hair. 'Everything's OK.'

But it wasn't.

I heard Matt's heart beating and then I heard footsteps.

'Oh God,' I said, breaking away.

Toby. On the stairs.

He clenched his fists and took a step towards us, his face furious. Hesitated, then spun round and went back the way he'd come.

What was I supposed to do now?

Stay? I looked at Matt.

Go? I looked up the stairs.

And then there was Rosa, putting her hand on the banister. Toby must've just passed her on the way up. 'There you are, Matt!' she said, peering at me. 'Hi, Daisy.'

She pulled a sympathetic face and motioned wiping away mascara smudges with her fingers. Her niceness just made the tears fall faster.

The trouble was, Matt wasn't mine to cry on any more.

Somehow I made it to the top of the stairs. I found Toby in the foyer, fishing his car keys out of his coat pocket.

'Don't go,' I said, reaching my hand out.

'I saw you with him. There's no point trying to deny it.'

'There's nothing to deny,' I said and my hand fell to my side as he moved away.

'God, I really thought you were different.' He was shaking his head as he pushed the exit door open. 'But you're all the same.'

I looked at Matt and Rosa, who were rounding the corner into the foyer. Then I watched Toby disappear through the door into the night.

And I ran after him.

CHAPTER 22

'Toby, wait! Wait!'

It was a lot harder to run in heels than football boots, but luckily he hadn't got far.

'What do you want?' he said, rattling his car keys. The street light glinted in his eyes and the chill air clouded his breath. He avoided the hand I stretched out.

'Just to talk.'

He made a short sound, halfway between a cough and a laugh. *Hah.* 'Talk. Right.'

Even with these skyscrapers on, he was taller than me. But not by so much I couldn't look him in the eye as I spoke.

'Toby, you need to stop being paranoid. I know and the stuff with your parents has done your head in, and Rhiannon hurt you, but —'

He'd started tapping his car keys against the palm of his hand now. 'Carry on,' he said through tight lips.

'I know you shouldn't try to change people,' I said. 'But sometimes maybe people *need* to change. Especially when it's just one thing that spoils everything. Look what you were like at the wedding and here tonight. People love you. Any girl would be beyond happy to be with you.' I hesitated and tugged my cardigan sleeves down in an effort to keep warm. 'I guess what I'm saying is you don't need to check up on me all the time. I would never cheat. I'm not like Rhiannon.'

His gaze travelled slowly, deliberately from my feet to the top of my head and he laughed again. A snarky, mean bark of a laugh. 'You can say that again.'

Maybe it was the street light, but with his mouth twisted in a sneer and those blue eyes hollowed out by shadows, his face looked completely different. Almost *ugly*.

'Whatever . . .' I exhaled loudly. 'Anyway, it was nothing. Like me giving Badger a hug because he was nervous. Or me talking to a wedding guest. Or some pervy lad bombing a photo. All of it – nothing. *Nothing*.' A cold blast of wind stung me and I wrapped my arms round myself.

There was a pause. Then he leaned in close, speaking slowly as if to a child. 'Have you finished now?' He grabbed my shoulders tightly. 'Have you?'

'Hey, let go!' I tried to shake him off, but it was like trying to shift stone.

He leaned right into me, sneering. 'Because, if you have, I could start telling you all the ways *you* need to change. And we could be here for a while.'

He shook me once and let go so suddenly that I staggered backwards. My ankle twisted over in the ridiculous sandals, then wobbling, windmilling my arms, *thud*, I was sprawled on the pavement, my leg in agony. The shock and the force left me breathless.

Toby stared at me for one, two seconds. Then he bent down, stretching his hand out. 'Oh my God, Daisy.' He said, voice all concern now. 'What did you do that for?'

I ignored his hand, wincing as I picked my handbag up and got first on my knees then to my feet by myself. Rapid footsteps were ringing through the darkness and I saw Ayesha storming up the road towards us.

'Daisyyyy!' she called.

Toby's expression had morphed to *worried*. 'Why are you wearing shoes you can't walk in? No wonder you fell over.' He reached towards me and I backed away.

'It's *always* better to be single than to date a twat,' I said out loud.

'What?' he said.

'Some advice from my friends,' I said, dusting down the back of my dress, 'which I think I'm going to take. Leave me alone, Toby.'

And I hobbled off towards Ayesha.

'Daze, are you all right? What's he done?' she said.

I was shaking now. 'I've twisted my ankle and I'm going to have to go home. He's definitely gone, right?'

She gazed behind me and nodded.

I refused to cry. 'Yeah, he's gone for good,' I said quietly. Then I flinched as pain shot up my leg again. 'You were right. I've been such an idiot.'

'What did he do?' she said as I leaned into her shoulder.

'He caught me talking to Matt and we had a row and, well, I should have listened to you. I'm sorry.'

'Let's go to the taxi rank,' she said, supporting me as we walked the mercifully few yards towards where the cabs were lined up. 'Wait here a mo while I get my bag.'

'I'm not going to let Toby wreck another night out,' I said, pausing to look her in the face. 'Seriously, go back to the party.'

She opened her mouth to argue but I wasn't backing down. 'I mean it, Ayesha. Just go, I'll be fine.'

'All right, if you're sure. I'll ring you later,' she said reluctantly. 'And Daisy, *please* don't see him again.'

'I won't,' I said, climbing into the cab. And I knew nothing would make me change my mind.

CHAPTER 23

Tap.

I woke in a panic.

Tap.

What the –?

Was someone tapping on my bedroom window? How?

Almost paralysed with terror, I crept to the window.

Tap.

A small white object pinged off the glass.

Wah! What *was* that?

I peered nervously down at the garden where a shadowy figure was standing.

Matt?!

I opened the window. A round white thing flew in and hit the sill. I picked it up, hesitantly sniffed, then took a tiny nibble. Leaned out.

'Matt, why are you throwing Extra Strong Mints at my house?'

'I tried gravel, but I didn't want to break the window,' he said in a loud whisper. 'They were all I had.'

'I meant what are you doing here?'

He coughed. 'I really need to speak to you.'

There was a click and then Mum's head poked out of the window next to mine. 'Hello, Matt,' she said staring down. 'How are you?'

'Oh, hi, Susie,' he answered with a little wave. 'Not bad thanks.'

'How's your mum?'

'Yeah, really good, thanks.'

'Glad to hear it.'

Huh?

I half expected to blink and see Matt in a ballgown, punting across a custard-filled swamp. Maybe the moon was a giant marshmallow. Or Mum was a talking horse. I turned to double-check, smacking my head on the window frame.

Ouch. Definitely not a dream then. Matt really was standing in our front garden at one in the morning chatting to my mum.

'Daze,' said Mum from her window, 'I think you should go down and let Matt in. Quietly though. Try not to wake River.'

Majorly bed-headed and wearing a pair of pyjamas old enough to leave home and start a family of its own, I tiptoed down the stairs. The frozen peas I'd put on my ankle had taken the pain down to a twinge. I unlocked the front door.

'Hey,' said Matt.

'Hey,' I answered. 'Come in.'

We sat on the sofa facing each other, Matt doing the lip-biting thing he always did when he was nervous.

'Well, this is weird,' he said.

I put a finger to my lips and gestured at the ceiling with my head.

'Sorry,' he said in a whisper. I shuffled up so I could hear him, feeling acutely aware that this was Matt. Here. Now.

'Wow, this is hard,' he said, lacing his hands together so his knuckles cracked. He shuffled up too and looked me directly in the eyes. He inhaled sharply.

'OK, the thing is I've missed you loads, Daisy, and I've decided I'm going to come home.'

The surreal I-must-be-dreaming sensation

intensified. 'I mean it,' he continued. 'I thought I was doing the right thing by going to Spain, but I wasn't. And when I saw you tonight with *him* . . .'

No mistaking the hate dripping off that word. 'Ayesha told me what happened outside.' Matt grabbed both my hands. 'Daze, I know I can't tell you what to do . . .'

He tailed off, but I knew where he was going.

'I'm not seeing Toby again,' I told him. 'No way.'

'Good,' he said, sinking back into the sofa a bit more. 'Because I want to come home so that things can be the way they were before, like I never left. Nothing's been right without you. It's like there's something missing.'

What the hell was this? It was as if his mouth had downloaded a transcript of Daisy's Favourite Fantasy Conversation. All those months dreaming of this moment and now it had arrived, I didn't know how to react.

'You never answered my calls or my emails and I thought you'd forgotten me, like that!' Matt snapped his fingers. 'And I thought, I need to let her go. But I couldn't, I *can't*, and what happened tonight just confirmed it. So I've decided, they'll have to manage at the bar. I can live with Dad and I'm going to see if I can go back to St Mary's. Or maybe come to your college.'

Letting this sink in, another thought struck me. 'What about Rosa?'

He shrugged. 'We had a thing for a bit, but there's nothing going on now. I mean, we're good mates, but it was obvious I wasn't really in to it and, well, she's kind of seeing someone else and I'm kind of here . . . with you.' He leaned in closer. 'And I know there's a million more things we need to say to each other, but all I can think about right now is how much I want to kiss you.'

Many, many thoughts were currently fighting for space in my head. Thoughts such as, *Ayesha was right about Toby. Matt's not seeing Rosa. Matt wants to move back home. Oh God, I'm going to kiss Matt.*

And also, *Oh God, I bet my breath could fell trees.*

'Really?' I said.

And then he kissed me.

CHAPTER 24

It was a perfect day for an autumn wedding. Blue, blue sky with the odd box-fresh fluffy cloud scattered about. Dad's voice came drifting across the courtyard at the local golf club. 'Thank you, if you could just move this way please. Lovely.'

He was lining the guests up against a spectacular natural backdrop of orange and scarlet trees. 'That's great. Smile!' he said.

'Daisy, have you seen the wig box?' asked Gemma, coming out of the clubhouse. 'I've set everything else out, but I can't find it anywhere.'

'I'll have another look in the van. Don't worry. It'll be around somewhere. Why don't you see if Badger needs a hand?'

She nodded and disappeared back to where Badger

and the rest of the band were setting up. I knew, after today, Mum and Dad would definitely be offering her the Saturday job. She was just perfect for Something Borrowed.

Above the heads of the wedding party, a faint vapour trail brushed a line of white in the blue. Maybe it was Matt's plane, I thought, though in reality his would be somewhere around Barcelona by now.

I yawned and rubbed my eyes, discreetly turning away from where the wedding party was gathering for champagne cocktails.

In some crazy reversal of the ultimatum I'd given him in June, I'd stayed up most of the night persuading Matt he needed to go back to Magaluf. His mum still needed him.

But we could just pretend the last few months never happened, he'd said.

I'd be lying if I said I wasn't tempted, but I said no. It wasn't the right thing to do.

These last few weeks with Toby had taught me lots of things, but mainly that at the moment I had to focus on settling into college and making friends.

Toby. Perhaps I should've been busy hating him, but, weirdly, I kind of felt sorry for him. But he'd gone too far, even though he was obviously so screwed up that he couldn't think straight. What a waste: to be so perfect and at the same time so flawed. I'd found a text when I woke up, asking if I'd let him explain.

My answer? **Please don't text me again.**

Maybe I'll call Brittany, see if she wants to go out tonight, flashed up straightaway.

I couldn't resist my fingers tapping back: **go for it.**

And then I blocked his number and tried hard to block him from my brain. I kind of thought he knew he'd gone too far.

I watched Mum and Dad now as they passed each other by the fountain, both smiling. Mum mouthed, 'Are you OK?' and I nodded, thumbs up.

They were so shocked when I finally told them about Toby. Next week they're coming into college to talk to someone about him. Mum says that Toby can't go around thinking that it's OK to act that way with girls, and I know she's right.

You could hire Something Borrowed to create your perfect wedding, but after that one special day, there were no guarantees. Our couples grew together or they grew apart. The test was how they faced the unknown future.

I was Mum and Dad's first big test, a tiny baby when they were only kids themselves. And they'd made it through.

As for me and Matt, Spain was our test. I knew now we'd always be friends, no matter what. And maybe we'd make it as a couple if we both wanted it enough. I could always visit him in Spain and we could pick up where we left off when he came home. And if either of us decided differently, well, then that would be OK too.

But I had a good feeling about us. There'd only ever really been me and Matt. Meeting Toby had proved that, in a weird way. And if there were any positives about the whole tatty mess with him, it was that I now knew moody brooding bad boys only ever work out in books. In real life, they just make you miserable. That was one mistake I would never make again.

I picked up the box with the last of the props and walked into a room filled with happy couples: Mum and Dad, Marv 'n' Harv, Gemma and Badger, and of course the bride and groom. They were all in pairs and I was on my own, but how could I feel lonely when I had my family and my friends?

And that was when it struck me: I could tell Ayesha and Beth I'd finally come up with Rule #10: *Single or* loved-up, as long as you're happy, it doesn't matter.

Simple as that.

And I smiled.

THE TEN RULES FOR GIRLS

#1 It is <u>always</u> better to be single than to date a twat.

#2 Always support your friends.

#3 Never change to please someone else.

#4 Don't hang around with people you don't actually like.

#5 Always be honest, even when it's painful.

#6 Dress to make yourself happy.

#7 Boyfriends are the icing, but girlfriends are the cake.

#8 Think positive.

#9 Rise above bitchiness (and if you can't, give it back better).

#10 Single or loved-up, as long as you're happy, it doesn't matter.

ACKNOWLEDGEMENTS

Massive thanks to Anne Clark and Stella Paskins and the teams at Egmont and Magellan for their hard work and incredible patience. Also Ross MacIntyre, Rebecca Fewster, Amanda Pawliszyn, Emma Swift and Molly Platt.

Thanks for support and encouragement from SCBWI North West.

To all the readers and bloggers who wrote to tell me how much they loved *Me & Mr J* and its international variations – that made me very, very happy. Thank you a million times.

Last, but never least, biggest hugs ever to Tim Bolton and Christian McIntyre.

THE #1 RULE FOR GIRLS

Sixteen-year-old Lara finds her soulmate.
There's just one problem – he's her teacher.

ME &
MR J

RACHEL McINTYRE